I WAS A TEENAGE CHEERLEADER

by
Aurelio O'Brien

This novel is a work of satirical fiction. Places, events, situations, and cultural references in this story are fabricated or highly fictionalized and any resemblance to actual people, living or dead, is coincidental.

Copyright © 2018 Aurelio O'Brien. All rights reserved.

No part of this book may be reproduced, stored in a retrieval system, or transmitted by any means, electronic, mechanical, photocopying, recording, or otherwise, without written permission from the author.

Bad Attitude Books, Altadena, California

ISBN: 978-1-935927-27-3

Beauty is only skin deep, but ugly goes clean to the bone.

Dorothy Parker

I'm not sure which woke me first, his snoring or the baby's cries. It was probably the baby's cries; I was used to his snoring. The evenly spaced, bass sax nose-solo never missed a beat, unperturbed by the raspy-shrill infant wailing in the next room. I smiled out a small huff, both exasperated and charmed. To be fair, he'd been up with Gena twice already, and although the actual production of her was far more of a cakewalk for him, he'd done his bit and then some before and since her arrival.

"Shhh, Gena honey, Mommy's here," I cooed as I entered the moonlit nursery, lofted her, and bounced her gently.

Gena's cries stopped with the very first bounce, as if controlled by a jiggle switch. She yawned and stared gape-eyed at me, or more accurately, through me, as if something far more interesting lay just beyond the back of my head. We settled in the armchair, I opened my robe, and Gena suckled contentedly.

It was my turn to yawn. Although her birth hadn't been easy, it wasn't as bad as I had feared. Three weeks since, I'd almost forgotten the pain, the memory of a six-hour labor being systematically erased by each moment of post-natal joy.

Through the window, a full moon bathed us in its diffuse glow. It was just above the window sill, making it appear unnaturally large.

Magical.

But not the nice fairytale magic that transforms pumpkins into coaches or transports you to Neverland, this was the harsher kind that morphs men into werewolves and awakens vampires to feed. I shivered, reminded of the power it once had—*real* power—over a scientifically rational skeptic of the supernatural like me.

I reached up and pulled the drapes closed, blocking it out.

I gazed down at Gena and wondered: would she have to go through what I went through? Could *she* be spared the dark side of that moon? Or would the sins of the mother be visited on the daughter? She had my red hair and fair skin, true enough, but she also had her father's blue eyes and square chin. Would her mixed heritage give her at least an even chance?

I reminded myself that I had once beaten that moon. But Artemis has a long memory. Would she now seek revenge? Extract a price...*at the expense of my daughter*?

I opened the drapes, stared defiantly at the silver orb, made a wish, and leaned in to kiss Gena firmly on her forehead.

Isn't that how your magic is foiled? With a kiss?

Janice Ian's lyrics popped into my head, as if to mock me and insist my child wouldn't escape the moon's magic just because I wished it so:

I learned the truth at seventeen,
That love was meant for beauty queens...

And suddenly, it all came rushing back, as if I were seventeen again...

Chapter One

THE INVISIBLE GIRL

I used to wonder if Autumndale actually got its name from the Autumndale Convalescent Home rather than the other way around. It was one of those preternaturally picturesque, sleepy, serene, older, self-contained suburbs that film location scouts love. Although we were now, by the calendar, better than mid-way through the 1970s, the general look and feel of our town appeared stuck in the late 1940s or early 50s. Our residential streets were dapple-shaded by tidy rows of mature maples, and in our downtown, a Googie malt shop aptly named The Malt Shop sat next to the deco-style neon-lit Crestview Theater whose owner had, so far, resisted the urge to split its one large auditorium into a multiplex.

This time-capsule environment had an equally abnormal effect on our residents. We were the Americana cliché. For example, at my school, Lawrence Talbot High, with its stately 1920s Romanesque Spanish revival architecture and functional bell tower, the football players were kings and the cheerleaders queens. We had the perfect central casting quota of geeks and pot-heads, with a decorative sprinkling of ethnic kids. The mostly-tenured faculty was traditionally, if not cartoonishly, eccentric. For example, the head of the English department, Mr. Toomey, wore a waxed handlebar mustache, cardigans, bow ties, and smoked a meerschaum pipe shaped like a mermaid—no kidding! The uniformed cafeteria ladies all protected their bee-hives under hair nets, and the librarian was—I'm not making this up either—a bespectacled spinster.

People normally feel they are the stars of their own internal biographical movies. With people like me, who possess a greater than normal sense of circumspection, it's not quite the same. I suppose years from now, when I reflect back on this time and my own internal movie version of it, I may decide to recast myself as the classically misunderstood "fish out of water" protagonist, but at the time I definitely saw myself as a hidden camera, merely observing it all (and even myself, at times) from the outside, my teenage life feeling safer from a distance, a thing to study and chronicle rather than actually live, something abstract rather than real.

I assume, to others, I was simply seen as Rhonda Glock, the brainy girl—that is, when they were actually *forced* to see me, for, to them, most of the time, I was invisible.

And invisibility is an asset when one doesn't wish to be seen.

Bud Langston opened his locker and re-sorted his daypack, stuffing some books in and pulling others out.

Not taking my invisibility completely for granted, I ducked behind the open metal door of my locker to observe him through one of the vent slots that had been bent wider by an earlier student who had probably forgotten his combination and had resorted to petty vandalism to pop the latch.

God.

Bud was perfect. He was proverbially tall, dark, and handsome well before any teenage boy had a right to be. I had convinced myself that, because he was the first-string quarterback, he was smarter than the rest of his brutish teammates—but then had to concede that even if true, it may not actually be saying much.

Especially after learning he needed a tutor for both math and science to keep his grades up. Any possible intellectual limitation on his part didn't stop me from making sure I got the job. It was a nice bit of machination. Being invisible means you overhear things and being clever means you can anticipate, so when I volunteered to tutor math and science mere *seconds* before Bud arrived in the tutorial center seeking exactly that, no one suspected a thing and chalked it up to serendipity.

Of course, Bud and I had already known each other forever. We had both grown up on the same block and had attended grade school and junior high classes together. We were even best friends as youngsters and played together all the time. But by the time junior high ended, and, as I more seriously pursued academics and he athletics, we drifted apart. And by the time we had reached Talbot High, we rarely even spoke.

But now I was spying on him. I could hear my heart pounding in my chest. I should have been smarter than this, *was* smarter, but it was no good. I had a crush on him, and crush is exactly what the word means; it grips you tight, and you cannot fight it, only submit. In the short two months I'd been tutoring Bud, my crush had mutated well beyond that initial involuntary-gooseflesh phase; its new mission was to convince me that Bud loved me back, and that we were meant for each other. When he said, "H'lo," to me in the halls, or called me, "Ron," instead of Rhonda, or phoned me at home in the evening to ask a *really* simple math question I was *certain* he must already know the answer to, the crush logged it as evidence of shared passion.

Scientific method, intellectual skepticism, rationality: all of my usual analytical tools blanched in the blinding sunburst of my crush's Harlequin Romance scenario.

He closed his locker, shouldered his daypack, and strode off. I couldn't stop myself from ogling his round and deeply-cupped buns as they flexed to and fro beneath his taut 501s, propelling him away, and I blushed at my own raw carnality.

This reverie was broken by raised voices spilling from Ms. Lyle's history classroom's open transom windows directly above my row of lockers. I couldn't make out all the words, only Ms. Lyle's professional matter-of-fact tone doing battle with an assertive, helium-voiced female student.

The door burst open, and the altercation moved into the hallway.

Again, I ducked behind my locker door to watch from the safety of my peep-slot.

It was Darleen Purdy who first flew from the room then spun back to continue arguing with Ms. Lyle. I had to suppress a snicker, because Darleen's spin was graceful despite her anger, even balanced on one toe, more like a dancer's pirouette than a spin. When her other foot planted, her pleated skirt and sunny blonde ponytail bounced a perfect coda, as if the action was all part of one of her practiced cheers, and my mind imagined her following it up with a leap into air-born splits.

"...but Miz Lyle, you've *got* to change my grade! Don't you see? You've just *got to*! If you flunk me, Miz Tarbo 'll *cut me from the squad!*"

"**And**, as I've *clearly* explained, I cannot do that, Darleen. It's too late. I've already filed my final grades. I warned you about this. **Several times**. You don't flunk a class overnight. You should have turned in all your homework on time and studied harder for the final. You'll have to repeat the class next semester, or pick it up in summer school."

"But, what about the class curve? Can't you just do a class curve?"

"Even if I did, it wouldn't help you," Ms. Lyle sighed, waving her off while making a beeline for the teacher's lounge door across the hall, and safety. "Rhonda Glock had perfect scores all semester."

The lounge door closed in Darleen's face.

Darleen stood frozen for a moment with her back to me. Her arms stiffened at her sides as her hands curled into tight fists. She inhaled deeply, turned, squared her pretty jaw and growled, "**Rhrrr-onda Gggg-lock**," through her Pepsodent-perfect, clenched teeth.

I had carefully inserted as much of me as would fit into my locker and pulled the door tight against me before Darleen turned and clipped past, for it was obvious she was convinced beyond a shadow of a doubt that I, Rhonda Glock, due to my perfect grades, had just ruined her life.

Chapter Two

BRAINS VS. BRAWN

As usual, I sat alone on the back steps of the science building and scarfed down my sack lunch before 12:30 so I could be in the Tutorial Center early. Usually Bud's tutoring session ran 20 minutes before the bell rang and I liked to have a little extra time to set up before he arrived. By setting up, I don't mean prepping to go over schoolwork; that I could do in my sleep. But...setting *me* up. That took effort. It took time to brush the frizz out of my disobedient hair and then angle a chair so the window light caught my best angle, and finally to check my reflection in the 1964 debate team's silver trophy platter displayed on the wall to make sure there were no bits of lunch stuck in my teeth.

But today, Bud was already there waiting.

"You're early," I blurted, stating the obvious in order to buy myself time as I repositioned my chair out of the window's direct glare and hoped to God my hair wasn't in bride-of-Frankenstein mode.

I ran my tongue over my teeth and sucked at them to dislodge any food before I turned to face him.

Bud smiled.

"I was anxious to see you."

My heart skipped a beat, but my head knew what he really meant.

"Ah. Your trig final."

He pulled the test from his binder and handed it to me. I sat and unfolded it. He had received an 89%.

"*Very* good," I pronounced professionally, while the fantasy me leapt up, threw her arms around him and kissed him proudly on the cheek, just shy of his left ear. If I kept this up, I'd mold Bud into my perfect brain-match in no time.

"What did you get?" he asked.

I squirmed.

"I did...fine."

"C'mon, what was your score?"

"I don't see the relevance...."

"Just tell me, Ron. Really, I can take it."

The fantasy me blanched and climbed under the desk as the real me momentarily froze. Before I got myself trapped in an infinite loop argument with the fantasy me, I simply confessed, "I...aced it."

Bud went limp.

"Look, Bud, learning is *not* a competition. It's not football, okay? And...test-taking has always been, well, easy for me. You can't expect to score as high as someone who spends all her time studying."

I watched Bud's broad, square shoulders slide further into a rounded droop.

"Besides, if I tried to throw a football, it'd get intercepted or something. We both have different natural talents. Your 89's a *great* score for a non-pro! You went from weak Cs to high Bs. That's a huge improvement!"

It seemed like his shoulders inched back up a bit, but I may have only imagined it.

"Anyway, looks like I'm out of a job now," I continued, smiling at him. "Unless you need help with something next semester?"

The fantasy me made the real me actually bat my eyes at him before she could be stopped. To cover, I batted them more, exaggerating my eye-flutters into the realm of cartoons.

Bud laughed and pulled out his new schedule,

giving it a glance.

"Hmm. Let's see...fortunately I expect to have a half-way-decent lab partner in Chemistry."

"*Half*-way-decent?"

"She's all right, I guess...."

Our eyes locked for a nanosecond before both of us averted them. For some reason Bud's eyes settled on my hands instead, and the fantasy me saw him reach out and take them in his own, lacing fingers.

"Of course, I could have used some help in biology *last* quarter, when we did sex-ed," Bud continued, shooting me an equally cartoony mock-leer back to break the moment.

I laughed but my cheeks felt hot.

"That's not my area of expertise," I vamped back, lips pursed in my best impersonation of our spinster librarian and an attempt to cover my embarrassment by playing along.

"You're blushing," he smirked, seeing through my act.

"Am not," I retorted, dropping my head so my hair hid my warming cheeks. I grabbed Bud's biology textbook as a diversion tactic and leafed it.

"We might as well use this time to prep for your next final."

"Ron? Can I say something...personal?"

"*May* I."

"Okay, *may* I say something personal?"

"No."

He ignored me and held up his trig test.

"Thank you for this, for helping me do this, Ron. Really. Getting into State next year is a huge deal for me, and with these kinds of grades, I've really got a shot."

Before the fantasy me could swoon, the brainy me bristled. Could Bud actually be so naive as to *not* see that his silly quarterbacking sports stats already made him a shoo-in for admission to *any* college of his choice, whereas my perfect 4.0 was still a crap-shoot?

"It's nothing," I lied. "Anyway, I get an extra credit for tutoring you. You have to practically discover a virus to make it into pre-med these days."

I glanced up. He looked a little stung by my glibness.

"*Aaanyway...*" I added, as our eyes locked again, "friends *should* help each other, no?"

This time Bud blushed.

"But, I mostly did it for the credit," I tossed off, uncomfortable with admitting to even friendly intimacy.

Bud's eyes stayed fixed on me and narrowed as he lit into a grin.

"Well, if it was just for the credit, then why...."

The door banged open, interrupting him and making both of us jump.

"There you are! I've been lookin' all over for you, man!"

There towered Durk, his raspy voice exorcising my onset of gooseflesh and Bud's grin.

Durk was, in a word, huge. I didn't know his last name, because no one, including the teachers, *ever* used it. He was the football-guy equivalent of Cher, I suppose, where only one name is sufficient, even though whatever Durk had done to merit this one name status was lost on me.

"Oh...hey, Durk," Bud stammered, his eyes blinking nervously.

Aha!

It then dawned on me that Bud had a double life, and the tutorial center and I were the one he wished to deny to the one he and Durk shared. I don't pretend to understand why team sports and academics are at war with each other, but they are and always will be—as certain as a zit on your nose the night of a prom.

Durk scanned the tutorial center as if he had just landed on an alien planet. Confusion rippled his testosterone-thickened monobrow. The center was set up in a dedicated, glass-partitioned library ell, and even though the glass door was clearly etched with, "TUTORIAL CENTER," the letters *were* reversed from the inside. One had to conclude, through observation, that Durk's brain was unable to decipher them.

He glanced at me, then at Bud.

"Whatcha doing here?"

"Uh, nothing," Bud stammered, stuffing his binder into his daypack. He shot a nervous glance at me, pasted on a practiced grin that could only convince a meathead like Durk, and turned back to him. "Why? What's up, man?"

"Darleen just got axed from the cheerleading squad. You know what that means?"

"Film at eleven?" I smirked.

"Huh?"

Bud stood and stepped between us; I wasn't sure if it was to protect me or hide me.

"What does it mean?" Bud asked.

"Replacement tryouts, Langston," Durk leered, "All the best lookin' babes 'll be in the gym at final period, dyin' to be rah-rahs, and itchin' to date football players."

I must have been wearing a look of disgust when Bud shot me a guilty glance. He masked it with that grin again and turned back to Durk.

"I should really hit the books after school, buddy. My bio final's tomorrow, and with practice and the games and all...."

"Man," Durk shot back in automatic-weapon cadence, bapping the sides of Bud's head with each word, "what-do-you-think-foot-ball-is-for?"

"People who enjoy getting hit in the head?" I offered.

Durk leaned his thick, neckless head around Bud in order to make eye contact, momentarily forced by his bruised male ego to acknowledge my existence.

"Very funny, Einstein-ette," he smirked, flashing the gap between his two front teeth. "We'll see who's laughing next fall, when I get a full scholarship from Yale or Harvard for passin' that pigskin around while all you book-grindin' albinos fight each other for what's left."

For a hyper-hormone-pumped near-gorilla, he was surprisingly canny.

"I stand corrected," I conceded with a flourish and a bow.

Durk shook Bud by the shoulders.

"Look, we're having a stellar season, man! A few more winning games and we'll both be swimmin' in scholarships. Live a little."

Durk flashed Bud a grin that I'd heretofore only seen on dogs, and just like a romping, slobbery, huggable lab, even I had to concede his grin carried a certain irresistible appeal.

"You are...sooo full of shit," Bud laughed, but he lofted his daypack and followed Durk to the door, prematurely ending our tutorial session and causing the fantasy me to burst into tears.

I leapt up to intercept Bud at the door, handing him his biology textbook back.

"Insurance," I reminded.

Thanks," Bud replied as he left with his arm around Durk's shoulder rather than mine.

Chapter Three

RAH RAH RAW

I left the library in no hurry to get to my next class: gym. I stopped at my locker and used my reluctance to go as an opportunity to tidy it before finally grabbing my gym bag.

Ugh. Gym. I hate gym—and I especially hated having it right after lunch, so on my way there I decided to track down Mr. Randall.

Mr. Randall taught senior civics, the only required class I had left to complete before graduation. And through a quirky series of clerical mess ups, I had not been able to schedule it yet. My numerous extra A.P. credits and straight As were useless unless and until I completed this one last stupid required class. And, despite my otherwise perfect GPA, they would hold my diploma hostage until I did finish it.

It was not because I was trying to avoid the class, but, once again at this semester's registration assembly, even though I raced to his table first, all Mr. Randall's classes for the coming semester were full. I had to promise my senior counselor, Ms. Swanson, to serve on her transfer student welcoming committee in order to now be armed with an official note stating that I had been approved by the principal to exceed Mr. Randall's class size limit—due to my senior status and special scheduling circumstances.

I spotted a quivering group of my sister schoolmates in the main hall and knew I had found my quarry: Mr. Randall, surrounded, as usual, by a flock of females. This was because Mr. Randall was young, good looking, and considered "cool." He wore his wavy brown hair just below his European-cut shirt's open collar. He alternately drove his MG roadster or rode his BSA motorcycle to work. These stereotypically masculine assets coupled with his authority-figure status and long sideburns meant many girls and a few of the lady teachers nursed major crushes on him. Mr. Randall was not only aware of his sexual allure, he reveled in it to the point of creeping out non-crushers like me.

It was also, I deduced, why his classes filled so quickly.

"If any of you young ladies need extra help before the final, I'm in my office between three and five," he stated, his eyes drifting down one of the more buxom girls' neckline.

I scowled and interrupted him, paper in hand.

"Excuse me, Mr. Rand...?"

The bell, in turn, interrupted me, and the girls reluctantly began to disperse. Mr. Randall barely glanced my way, mostly noting, it seemed to me, my smaller-than-average bust, and started off down the hall.

Apparently, my inadequate bust size had rendered me invisible to him?

Grrrr...

I pursued.

"Excuse me! Mr. Randall...?"

"Not now, please. Didn't you hear the bell? I'm in my office, three to five."

"But, Mr. Randall, I've been trying to get into your civics class since early last year. It's the only required class I have left before I graduate this fall. I realize your classes are already full, but this semester's my last chance."

He kept up his stride without slowing, so I quickened mine to get in front of him. Walking backward, I held the note up to his face, forcing him to stop.

He snorted and ran a hand though his curly locks.

"Ms. Swanson cleared it with Principal Cummings for me to join your third-period class, but I'll need your signature."

Mr. Randall scanned the note, then me, brushing both aside.

"Sorry, the class is full. Ms. Woodley is offering the course during summer school. I'm sure she'll have plenty of room."

He resumed his clip and I continued my pursuit.

"But I graduate *this* year. Please, Mr. Randall..."

He ducked into the staff men's room, stopping me in my tracks. I debated following him in when I heard the lock click.

"What an a-hole," I muttered, as I stalked off to gym.

I entered the girl's locker room and made a beeline for a free locker to quickly throw on my gym clothes. Most of the other girls were already changed and waiting for class to start, and although I only realized this in retrospect because my mind was still stewing on what an absolute jerk Mr. Randall was, they were all a-chatter about Darleen Purdy flunking world history and being cut from the cheerleading squad. Talk was ambitious, with many vowing they would rise up to take her place.

It is remarkable to think that, what with children starving in Ethiopia, the oil crisis, the Cold War, and genocides in Uganda, a vacancy in the cheerleading squad was the number one topic of discussion at Talbot High that day, but such was the insular nature of the mentally bleak social terrarium I was trapped in.

But really...who was I to judge anyway? My current priority was how to manipulate Mr. Randall into admitting me into a class I didn't really care about so I could get a nearly worthless diploma in order to finally pursue something I really *did* care about. And, in the grand scheme of things—*honestly*—is that any more justifiable or valid than shaking about a pair of pom-poms? No, none of us escapes jumping through the lame hoops required to achieve what passes for a successful high school education.

What did finally distract me from my brooding was the locker room suddenly quieting to the dead-still silence of a nunnery crypt. I had my tee shirt up over my head at that exact moment, so I paused and listened. The quiet was cut by the click of the outside door closing, followed by petite-but-determined footfalls headed in my direction. They stopped.

I pulled my tee shirt down to see Darleen Purdy's furious face inches from mine.

"You...**bitch!**" she screeched, close enough for me to feel the heat of her Tic Tac fresh breath.

I backed away.

"*You, you...***GEEK!**"

I backed further away, and decided to play dumb.

"Excuse me, Darleen, but...what's your problem...?"

"*You're* my problem! You ruined my life! I'm cut from the squad and it's all your *fault*! You just had to get a *hundred* on everything—I hate you! I hate you, ***I HATE YOU...!***"

One of the other girls giggled nervously.

Darleen spun around to face a gathering semicircle of girls.

"Don't any of you laugh! I've always lived up to the Cheerleader's Creed. Other girls didn't, but I did!"

Darleen smiled sweetly and recited, almost as if in a trance:

*"Every girl who's pure of heart,
Is pretty, clean, and neat,
May be a member of the squad,
If these four rules she'll meet:*

*"She must be cute,
She must have spirit,
And sports must be her God.
She mustn't ever fail a class,
Or she'll be off the squad."*

Her smile melted to a moue as she finished the last line. She spun back to face me, on one toe again, with her hair and dress bouncing after, the perfection of this move only marred by the snarl directed squarely at me now curling her pink-glossed lips. A mascara-darkened tear rolled down her cheek, making me *almost* feel sorry for her.

"But...w-why blame me?" I stammered, while glancing about for any potential escape route.

"You couldn't be satisfied with just an A," she sputtered back, "You had to get a hundred on *everything*! Ruin the class curve! RUIN MY LIFE!"

She launched herself airborne, like a pouncing cat, and before I could suck a startled breath, she was atop me, gripping my hair and shoving me face-first onto the musty concrete floor, where she sat on my back pounding away with her dainty fists.

"Get...this...lunatic...off of me!" I screamed between punches, but none of the other girls came to my rescue.

Instead, they circled tighter to chant:
"FIGHT! FIGHT! **FIGHT!**"

My adrenaline surged. I pushed up and managed to topple Darleen and wriggle free of her. I scrambled on all fours working my way to my feet, and dashed for the safety of a vacant toilet stall. I almost made it too, but Darleen caught hold of my wrist. My arm remained exposed, sandwiched in the stall door, and before I could wrestle it in with me, I felt a sharp pain rip through it.

Several of the girls gasped and one squealed.

I loosed a blood-curdling scream that mixed with Darleen's angry growl; our echoing voices eerily melding into a singular howl more apt to be heard on safari than in a girl's locker room; it was raw, physical, bestial.

Mixed in with the stabbing pain in my arm was an odd jolt of pleasure, which made no sense to me at the time—like the adrenalin rush you get when you crest that first big hill on a roller coaster, or when everyone leaps out at you at the start of a surprise party—but I was in no state of mind to analyze it.

As our tandem howl faded, it was replaced by Coach Tarbo's voice, barking orders.

"Break it up, girls!"

I felt us both collapse to the floor together, me in agony and Darleen in spent resignation.

Darleen loosed her grip and I retracted my arm.

I almost fainted when I actually saw it; she'd bitten deep into my forearm, opening a half-moon shaped flap of tissue. My vision tunneled, and I instinctually clapped my free hand over the wound to press the flap back in place and stem the bleeding, before wailing anew.

"All right, girls! I said, **break it up!**" I heard Coach Tarbo scold, clapping her hands together with a couple of sharp cracks. "Show's over! Hit the track! **NOW!**"

The scamper of footfalls echoed away. When my head cleared I teetered up and elbowed open the stall door.

Darleen lay in a heap outside it, sobbing and mumbling incoherently. Her ponytail had come loose from its little band with the pink plastic balls, and her usually silken hair now resembled an explosion.

Coach Tarbo placed a tender hand on Darleen's shoulder, helping her up.

"There, there. Come on, dear," she said, urging Darleen to a bench.

"Hello!?" I growled, as blood oozed from between my fingers and down my wrist to pool on the floor next to me, my anger the only thing keeping me from passing out, "May *I* get a little help, Coach! I'm the one bleeding here!"

Coach Tarbo left Darleen and crossed the room to grab one of the clean shower towels.

She returned and wrapped it tightly around my wound.

"I swear you girls are worse than the boys. You're both going on report," she announced, "and I'll have no arguments!"

Her reprimand was cut short as all three of us jerked and gasped, because suddenly, as if out of thin air, a wraith appeared at the stall door: frizzled gray-brown hair tucked up in a sweat-stained John Deere cap, overalls mottled by iron-on patches, an open, faded-blue smock rolled up at the sleeves, and a bucket and mop in hand. Embroidered in ironically lacy script across her smock was the name Lainey. Talbot High's ancient custodian rarely came out during the day, when students were around, and yet, here she was, her back hunched, and with a face like an apple-head doll.

Her ancient, jet-black Chihuahua, Dinah, padded out from behind her, its unclipped nails clicking on the concrete floor of the locker room. Rumors of unspoken administration crimes known only to Lainey were rife at Talbot High to explain why that creepy little canine who followed Lainey everywhere must have received some sort of special dispensation to be allowed to wander the campus unleashed.

Dinah clicked up and sniffed my blood, then raised its cataract-hazed, milky green eyes to stare straight at me, connecting the smell.

"Get back, Dinah," Lainey ordered, then drenched her mop, squeezed it in the mechanical ringer attached to her wheeled bucket, and covered the pool of blood with it, working it from side to side, as if cleaning up blood was simply routine.

"I swear, Lainey, you must have a sixth sense," Coach Tarbo remarked after regaining her composure.

Dinah continued to stare me down, motionless, like she'd been flash-frozen; I had to look away and let her win.

"Better take that to the nurse," Coach Tarbo said, nodding at my arm, then leaned over and lifted Darleen off the bench, helping her into the gym office with a, "There, there, dear. Come in and rest a bit. I know. I know. You've had a rough day."

Chapter Four

LOSERS, WEEPERS

Walking to the nurse's office, I felt both numb and dumbfounded. Not just from the shock of Darleen's brutal assault, but because none of it made any sense at all. Was I crazy, or was everyone else? Darleen had just tried to bite a chunk of flesh out of me, so why was she the focus of Coach Tarbo's sympathy?
*Because she's **pretty**?*
Was it more tragic that pretty little Darleen would no longer be able to jump up and down like an idiot at rallies than for me to have my arm ripped open and permanently scarred by a lunatic? Being stripped of her treasured pompoms was a bigger deal than me lying in *a pool of my own blood?*
I crossed campus in my gym clothes with my arm wrapped in the towel, hoping my powers of invisibility held fast. I never felt comfortable in the gym short-shorts they made us wear, with so much of my pale thighs on display and my nipples more obvious through the sports bra and tee.
Fortunately, classes had begun and the campus was deserted.
I sighed. I was beginning to see there was a big downside to this invisibility thing. It meant people like Darleen got all the attention. *Why?* Obviously because she looked cute and bouncy and perky and could fill a sweater better than I could. But...how stupid is *that?* Why does everyone put so much value on just being pretty? We attend school to learn, don't we? So, why was I blamed, ridiculed, looked down on, and

even physically attacked for getting good grades, for demonstrating my innate intelligence? For actually succeeding at what was supposed to be the primary task at hand?

I insisted to myself that this kind of insanity only exists in high school, and that high school isn't the real world. It didn't work. Durk's earlier accurate assessment of the college application process reminded me that, although some of the pieces might get shuffled around, college, and *yes*, even the work-a-day world beyond it would merely be other versions of same cockeyed game.

"Am I nuts?" I asked myself, this time muttering the question aloud, "Or is everyone else?"

The question was rhetorical and it didn't really matter which answer I chose. Either way, I was the one out of step. In the battle between beauty and brains, brains don't stand a chance. Nope, brutish boys and pretty girls: they rule the roost. *Everywhere.* It was insane, but there it was. There was no way for me to force sanity on everyone else, and—let's face it—I would *never* be considered a beauty. On a hundred-point scale I'd probably land only a bit above the middle on a good day, and if I combed out my hair, went on a diet, and got a little sun I might eventually hit the low 70's, maybe. But I was used to top scores, and anyway, this beauty thing seemed to be more or less pass-fail.

I entered the nurse's office and was slapped with the pungent smells of Pine-Sol and rubbing alcohol. I took a seat in one of the stackable chairs lined up against the wall, as far away as I could from a freckle-faced, wimpy freshman boy with a round brown metal waste bin clamped between his knees. He was the same sickly-green color as the office walls.

"I threw up in woodshop," he explained without my asking.

A short, chubby sophomore girl, whose name I didn't remember, even though she had been in the same gym class with me all semester, sat between us, fidgeting.

Nurse Weld came out from behind a curtained room divider where she kept her desk, flipping through a ledger. She stopped on a page, wrote something down, and handed the girl a sanitary napkin.

"Josephine Kent. This is the *third* time you've had your period this month, and funny, it always hits right before gym class," she said, pointing to a page in her ledger, "I've been keeping track."

Josephine's mouth gaped and her eyes clicked back and forth as if searching her brain for a way to explain the inexplicable.

Nurse Weld didn't wait for it.

"Back to gym class," she growled, and Josephine dashed out.

"Who's next?"

Since the green kid had just stuffed his head into his waste bin, dry-heaving, and I was bleeding and would probably need to be sent to the hospital for stitches—and maybe even a rabies shot—I raised my good hand and took cuts.

"What's the problem, honey?"

I held up my arm wrapped in the bloodied towel. Nurse Weld motioned.

"Put it in the sink."

I rose and stood over the large porcelain sink in the corner of the room and Nurse Weld followed, attacking the wrapping with all the delicacy of a longshoreman.

"*Aaak*," I mewled and pulled back. "Let me do it."

"Suit yourself," Nurse Weld sighed, while I gingerly unwrapped the clotting layers of thin terry. The gym towels were so cheap and small they were useless for drying off after a shower, being closer to the size of hand towels than bath towels. I cringed as I slowly pulled the final layer of cloth loose from the wound; the minute I saw my bloodied arm, I got light-headed again. I gripped the sink edge and averted my eyes.

Nurse Weld took a small squeeze bottle of peroxide solution from a shelf above the sink and fizzed away the lumps of clotted blood while my vertigo slowly abated.

She finally daubed the arm with some gauze, then snorted.

I looked down.

My arm was unmarked. The wound, *gone!*

Vanished.

Completely.

"Nice try, kid," Nurse Weld laughed. "You would've gotten further with the time-o'-the-month excuse."

My mouth opened to speak, but I was struck dumb. I reached out to prod my own forearm, unable to believe what I saw. It was intact. No sign of injury. No open flap of flesh, no teeth marks, no blood.

Nothing.

"What you girls won't do to get out of gym," Nurse Weld sighed, opening her ledger to a fresh page, "but all it does is end up getting you on report. So, what's your name...?"

But I was already out the door.

I ran full tilt all the way back to the locker room, wondering: Had I lost my mind? Was I hallucinating?

Was this whole day an elaborate dream and I was actually still at home, in bed, asleep?

But everything in front of me seemed perfectly normal. Rational. Real.

The locker room was deserted when I got there.

I approached the bathroom stalls, still panting, trying to catch my breath. No sign of blood. No sign of Lainey. No creepy little dog.

The floor was clean and dry.

I crossed to Coach Tarbo's office door and peered in through its small, wire-meshed window. The lights were out. No one was inside. No Coach. No Darleen.

No one, anywhere.

I held up my arm to the light.

Yup. Intact. Every last freckle in place.

I stood frozen. Incapacitated. Completely undone.

My rational mind simply could not wrap itself around the information my eyes were sending it.

And then, *kerzap-p-p*, the P.A. system squawked to life, jumping me out of my skin.

"Attention! Attention!" The school secretary's sharp voice echoed through the empty locker room, "All girls participating in tryouts for varsity cheerleader, please report to the gymnasium."

As she repeated the message, I burst out laughing.

Not because it was all *that* funny—it was, perhaps, ironically timed—but when the mind doesn't know what to do with itself anymore, it tends to laugh, and that's what mine decided to do just then.

Not just a little laughter, either. A lot of laughter. But I couldn't stop laughing. In fact, my whole body was slipping out of my control. My skin quivered all over. I felt as if I was shrinking inside myself, soon only able to look out through my eye sockets, as if they were my bent locker door slot. Really only observing and no longer participating.

My body continued heaving with laughter, my hysterics changing with each inhale into a higher and higher-pitched giggle, and it felt alien, because I was never the least bit prone to giggling. And the more I giggled on, the less I sounded like me.

Fear gripped me when my body doubled-over all on its own, still giggling away, then more convulsively, like in the throes of a fit, or a seizure, and I collapsed to the floor. I was all body and emotion; my mind, my thoughts weren't connected to any of it. Then bang, I was jolted by a sharp, prolonged spasm of pleasure mixed with pain. It was the exact same odd combination of sensations I felt the moment Darleen bit me, but this time more intense, more continuous, and not just at the bite site, but everywhere. Every nerve ending quivered with pleasure and pain. I felt each one of my hair roots, every pore, every individual cell of my body all at once, as if they'd all been simultaneously electro-shocked wide awake and were dying to come out and play.

The trill of my now pneumatic giggles was soon joined by soft, moist, crunching sounds, and I glanced down in horror to see my legs eerily lengthen and deform before my eyes, widening at the calf and narrowing at the ankle. In the full-length mirror near the shower stalls I could see my cheekbones raise and protrude with more gentle crackles of bone and squish of sinew. My eyeballs swelled too, while the space between them widened. It was terrifying, but mesmerizing. I watched my facial features drift, readjusting themselves into a perfect, ideal female heart-shape, while my hazel irises faded into larger, sky-blue pools, and the lashes surrounding them lengthened and multiplied. I saw my untidy mass of frizzy red hair relax and lighten—as if floating in a stream—into a soft, silky, golden-blonde mane of large, long, sinuous curls. My breasts enlarged, filling my sports bra to capacity, and I heard myself giggle all the louder at that, because it was all too funny, and well, yeah, *scary* too, but mostly funny...*wasn't it?*

I pulled my tee shirt up to see my heretofore impossibly stubborn paunch of baby fat there melt, cinch, and lengthen into abdominal perfection, both toned and girly-soft, every complex curve of it making a lovely transition into the next, and saw my new delicate, slenderer hands knot the bottom of the tee just under my breasts in order to show it off.

And there, next to me on the floor, lay Darleen's lost hair band, with its two little pink plastic balls at each end of its cloth-clad elastic and I giggled afresh, hearing myself perk, "Finders keepers, losers weepers," but it wasn't my voice anymore—it was far too lilting and sugary.

I plucked up the hair band and stood, finally taking in a full-length view of the physically confident, stunning beauty I'd become. I was Gidget, and Lolita, and Tammy, and Barbie, and Aphrodite, all rolled into one. I absolutely gushed girlish youth and teen-fresh estrogen.

I was...*adorable.*

I bunched my new glossy, spun-gold mane up tight to the crown of my head, double-looping and securing it in the band, and then spun myself around on one toe in a pirouette, stopping my spin to face the mirror again, and grinned to myself when my pony tail bounced after in a perfect coda.

And, with another giggle and just for the heck of it, I leapt into air-born splits, completely tickled with myself.

But...where the hell was *I*? Not in control of this new body, even though I felt everything it felt. This wasn't really me, was it? It had to be some sort of hallucination or dream. Yet, it felt utterly real, and I felt so *good*, so worry free, so physically healthy, so full of positive energy, and so completely alive. I didn't feel like my usual self at all. I certainly didn't look, act, or sound like me either. So, when I skipped out the door toward the gym without a second thought, the small part of me still left inside, staring out through my now larger blue eyes, had absolutely no idea what this new me might do next.

Chapter Five

INSIDE OUT & UPSIDE DOWN

I skipped into a gymnasium teaming with fidgeting, preening, giggling, and artistically posed would-be cheerleaders of every kind. Chills ran down my spine and gooseflesh prickled my limbs. I was so excited! Wafts of Jungle Gardenia and Chanel No.5 filled the air. Girls dressed in short pleated skirts, or tight short-shorts and even tighter sweaters or tee-shirts practiced their turns and cries, waving their pompoms and batons all about. Along one wall, perched on tiered risers, conferring in earnest as they evaluated each girl's charms, was the football team, rating the dateability of any potential future game day, rally, and possible prom co-participants. Opposite the footballers, across the court, were arrayed the current cheerleading team, conferring in earnest while weighing in the balance the possible competition for boyfriends against having a competent addition to their squad.

Seated beneath a basketball hoop, behind a folding table at the far end of the gym were the gimlet-eyed judges, faces inscrutable as the tryouts proceeded: Coach Tarbo, assistant girls' coach, Ms. Strangio, and Felicia Chao, the head cheerleader. The squeals, giggles and sis-boom-bahs of the hopefuls competed with the aid of an audiotape of the Talbot High fight song playing over the gym's speaker system. A serpentine queue of hopefuls progressed across the gym floor toward these arbiters of their future.

I felt myself check the knot in my tee shirt, wet my lips, adjust my shorts to better cup my now rounder behind, and I marveled how natural it felt to smile with my teeth showing. I could feel everything this new me did as if it was simply me doing it all, because it *was* me, but I didn't seem to have any control over my own actions, so for the moment I made no effort to participate or intervene, only watch from inside. As I pondered whether I actually could exercise *any* real physical control over myself anymore or not, I tried glancing at the risers and found that I could do so, although moving around in this new self felt rather like it does when one is in a dream; I seemed able to exercise only the vaguest effect over my own actions.

Durk stood up in the stands. The big ape was hard to miss, and he seemed to be trying to get *my* attention, which puzzled me until I recalled what I now looked like. I then noticed Bud sitting next to him, his nose in his biology text.

Good for him.

A roar of laughter burst out from the risers as students, apparently desperate for entertainment, were following the competition. I felt my head jerk loose from my control to catch Marnie Lemon, one of the drama girls, finish her emotive cheerleading audition by tipping over on her butt with a loud thud after a failed attempt at splits.

I felt myself giggle and coo a sympathetic, "Aww," then clap for her effort.

The girl in front of me heard me and turned.

I recognized her: Tanya Sweet. Her name was fitting, because even though she was one of the pretty, popular girls I usually hate and who should have hated me back, she had never made me feel completely invisible when I was around her.

"Hi," she said, and held out a hand, "I'm Tanya."

I spontaneously giggled at the fact that she didn't

recognize me, but my new outer self took control, shook hands, and perked back, "Hi, I'm Ronnie."

Ronnie...? It felt automatic, you know, like cutesy girls dotting the i's in their names with little hearts or daisies. Tagging a "y" or "ie" on the end of a name adds extra cuteness if one's name doesn't already come equipped: June becomes Junie, Barbara, Barbie.

Now, *apparently*, I—tada!—became Ronnie.

"I've never seen you around here before. Are you new?" Tanya inquired.

I felt my head bobble affirmatively as Ronnie answered, "Uh-huh, this is my first day!"

It was true enough.

I glanced down at the pompoms in Tanya's left hand and Ronnie sighed, "Oh, darn."

"What's wrong?" Tanya asked.

"I don't have any pompoms."

Tanya lofted hers and twirled them, thinking. Then, she smiled at me.

"Well, when I'm done, you can borrow mine."

"Oh, yay! Thanks, Tanya!" Ronnie said, and hugged her.

Tanya hugged back. The hug felt surprisingly genuine despite the fact that Tanya probably would have never hugged the real me, and I would have never ever hugged any of my fellow students—except maybe Bud, if ever I had the opportunity.

But Ronnie was running the show now and she was gregarious.

The line moved swiftly, thanks to Coach Tarbo, Ms. Strangio, and Felicia cutting off all the obviously unqualified girls before they finished.

I had no idea what *I* would do when I got up there, but thanks to Ronnie, I felt an utter fearlessness despite being unprepared. I marveled at how easy life felt while bathed in Ronnie's vapid confidence; the bliss of ignorance without any anxiety over the potential folly that wisdom might suggest, and I pondered how a cerebral person like me might adopt this devil-may-care attitude without having to have a complete lobotomy first.

I felt myself spontaneously wresting control again when I glanced back to see what Bud was doing now. Durk caught my glance and assumed I was looking at him, so he waved to me. Much to my horror, Ronnie waved back, even jumping up and down enthusiastically as she did.

There was an obvious a downside to her vapidity.

Durk nudged Bud and pointed my way.

Bud looked up and finally spotted me. He tilted his head with interest, so *I* waved to him, but the next second, Ronnie jerked my head back to the front of the gym to watch and cheer on Tanya's routine.

Tanya was good, maybe great; she stuck her landing from a final front handspring, with her feet locked together and pompoms raised. The approval from the crowd and the squad granted her the edge over all the rest.

She skipped to the sideline as Ronnie applauded and squealed her own approval, and Tanya tossed me her pompoms with a wink.

Felicia rewound the music for me, and on the upbeat, I felt Ronnie launch my body head over heels into a series of handsprings that ended in a full front flip with a twist, then a somersault into a stand, on tippy-toe, to create the "T" for Talbot with my arms held rigidly out to my sides in perfect sync to the school song's lyric. I willingly ceded all control to her, even happy to be along for the ride, smitten with my own new deftness, athleticism, and grace. I recalled reading that people who witnessed the first a-bomb test marveled at the sheer beauty of it, that, as scary as the moment was, it actually created colorful rainbows as it ripped the atmosphere wide open, and that is exactly how this moment struck me. How could Ronnie, this mushroom cloud of cute, how could she come out of *me?* But here *I* was, doing leaps, spins, and cartwheels while Tanya's pompoms arced overhead to land neatly back in my hands as I ended my routine with a dramatic drop into sideways splits on the last drumbeat.

The gym erupted in applause and cheers, and the next thing I knew Felicia and the rest of the squad had me lofted in the air to parade around the room, welcoming me as the newest member of the cheerleading the squad, and gifting me with Darleen's uniform and pompoms.

I was glad to see Tanya was among those clapping for me, bearing no ill will for my having beaten her, as Ronnie tossed her back her pompoms and blew her air-kisses and pantomimed, "I'm sorry," to her through the roar of the crowd.

On the way out of the gym, Durk and Bud awaited me by the door.

Durk stepped into my path, expanded his already gorilla-sized chest, and extended a meaty hand.

"Durk's the name. Tight end."

"Ronnie," she giggled back, daintily shaking his thick mitt, while I struggled with all my might to wrest control from her before she said or did anything really stupid.

"I haven't seen you around before," Durk continued, his eyes dancing about my body.

"This is my first day."

The wrestling match inside my own head

resulted in nothing more than finally getting Ronnie to look at Bud instead, and in a confused voice, she muttered, "Don't I know you from...*somewhere?*"

"I don't think so. I'm Bud," he replied. I felt him take my hand. He looked directly into my eyes with the glazed look of one completely smitten, and I swooned back, and in the process ceded any control I had to Ronnie again.

"Bud. That's a funny name," she giggled back, making me feel like a complete idiot and I felt Ronnie blush for me.

The final school bell rang.

"Well, gotta change now, bye guys!" Ronnie announced, bouncing toward the door.

"Wait!" Bud exclaimed, jumping between me and the door. He scrawled something on the corner of a paper, tore it off, and handed it to Ronnie. "I'd like to see you...maybe...sometime...."

Ronnie tucked the note into my cleavage.

"See me...? Here I am!" Ronnie replied, striking a perky, *16 Magazine* teen model pose, adding a little, "Voila!" and a giggle, then, "That's French, you know," leaving the two boys frozen and agape.

And with a toss of my ponytail and cute little backward wave over my shoulder, she skipped us off to the locker room.

Chapter Six

WIGGING OUT

The next thing I remember, I was slumped on the edge of a toilet seat in one of the locker room stalls. I felt physically exhausted, but with a slight endorphin high, like I had just finished running a full marathon. I instinctually checked my arm again to see if the bite mark had returned.

It hadn't.

I felt my bust; the same as usual; then pulled a hank of my hair in front of my eyes to see if it was its usual reddish frizz.

It was.

I emerged into the steamy locker room, rubbed the closest mirror with the palm of my hand to clear it, and stared hard at myself.

Yup.

My pale, oval face, hazel eyes, stupid cupid's bow lips, and freckle-specked nose stared back. My eyebrows furrowed and my lower lip pouted out in disappointment. *Oh, it's just me,* I thought, which immediately irked me and I scowled back at myself for my spontaneous disappointment of *not* seeing Ronnie's prettier-than-mine face staring back at me, confirming that I was just as superficial as all the rest of my silly schoolmates.

But, have I been in the toilet stall this whole time? Was it all just some sort of weird daydream? Was any of it real?

I scanned the locker room.

Nothing seemed out of step. Other girls showered

and dressed, oblivious to me, as usual. I was invisible again, and the comfortable familiarity of it convinced me that none of it could have possibly happened for real: there was no bite, no transformation, no cheerleading audition, none of it.

I sighed, relieved.

I guess I must have dreamt the whole thing while asleep in that toilet stall, I concluded, with a shrug. It was the only logical answer, *but, jeez...how weird is that?*

I returned to my locker, lost in confused thought, opened it, and immediately slammed it shut again with a loud bang.

"Something wrong?" Tanya Sweet asked from the other end of the locker aisle, tucking her lovely auburn hair behind one ear to get a better look at me.

I turned to her, pasted on a smile, and laughed, "No, I...nothing. Thanks for asking, ah...Tanya."

She scanned me a moment, then rolled her eyes at what I guess she took to be my terminal weirdness and went back to dressing herself, and I, of course, felt like a complete idiot. Maybe Tanya's last name wasn't so apt after all, but...could I blame her?

I sat on the bench facing my gym locker and slowly cracked it opened again.

There, neatly folded inside, lay Darleen's cheerleading uniform and pompoms.

Before the other girls could see, I stuffed them into my gym bag, zipped it closed, and began changing back into my street clothes.

As I removed my sports bra, a torn slip of paper fell out.

I picked it up and unfolded it. It was the top of an algebra test, with an all-too-familiar phone number scrawled across it.

The test's score was an 89%.

"Oh, God..." I wheezed, and had to sit again.

I pulled the family station wagon into our driveway, stopped, put the transmission in P, set the parking brake then sat motionless for a moment with my hands gripping the wheel. I took several deep, slow breaths.

In front of me, set back from our shady street, sat our calm, off-white, two-story, 50's contemporary, with its muted-blue trim and pink azalea-hedged entry, like a page from a children's picture book. My entire otherworldly afternoon again seemed to fade away.

"No," I stated aloud. "I can't accept it. It's *impossible*."

I collected my book bag, gym bag, binder, and stack of textbooks, closed the car door with my butt, fumbled with my keys to lock it, and made my way to the front door.

I had to press my bundle against the door to free up a hand, but before I could turn the knob, someone opened the door from the inside, tipping me into the foyer.

Books, binders, and bags spilled across the flagstone floor; but I was able to stagger back my balance, only to be sent reeling again at the sight before me: a mismatched pair of miniature, munchkin, drag queens, each with one hand on his hip and the other waving tiny circles in the air from his wrist.

"Can we *twalk?* Can we *twalk???*" they both aped in heavy Brooklyn accents.

"You brats," I groused, "You scared me half to death!"

"Oh, grow up, you walking bwarf bag," Richie,

the older of my two younger brothers, vamped in a high-pitched rasp.

"We're not supposed to be scary, we're supposed to be *glamorwous*," Robbie, the younger of the two, explained, following with a hoarse, "Am I gworgeous or what...?"

Robbie primped his wig, pursed his red, lipstick-drenched mouth, and wiggled his padded hips while Richie snapped pictures of him with our Dad's camera.

"Gworgeous, are you kidding...?" Richie replied with a smirk, "You look like roadkill."

"That's because I look like you, honey."

"Richie, what *are* you two *doing?*"

"We're entering the Joan Rivers look-alike contest."

"It's in *The Enquirer*," Robbie explained, holding up the tabloid to show me.

"You know Mom hates it when you read that stuff," I scolded, but had to work hard to look stern and not laugh so I wouldn't further encourage them.

"Mom also says it's better to read than watch TV," Robbie countered.

"And have you seen *Mom's* show lately?" Richie added.

"Bwooooooooring!" they both Joaned.

"It's worth the risks," Richie explained, "First prize is *five hundred dollars*..." He stopped himself to look me up and down before adding, "Hey! We should enter **YOU!** C'mon! We'll split the money!"

"Yeah!" Robbie chirped, also sold on the idea.

"I've had enough dressing up for one day, thank you very much," I muttered while collecting my things from the floor and piling them on the landing.

I turned back to face my cross-dressed brothers, and sighed.

Why couldn't I have a normal family? Today of all days?

Then, a light dawned. My brothers had raided Mom's clothes closet to make themselves up like this. And were wearing her expensive, real-hair wigs left over from her blond phase. *And* Richie donned one of her best cocktail dresses to boot. If Mom found out, there'd be hell to pay, and it was certain, rather than likely, that I, as their elder sister, would, in the wonderful world of twisted adult-logic, be the one ultimately responsible for *all* of it.

I reached out and snatched off Robbie's wig. It was rock-hard.

Ohmygod! What did you do to Mom's wig?" I wailed.

"It's just hair spray. We had to style it," Richie defended.

"You *wha...*?" I closed my eyes and silently counted, not making it even to five before I snapped, "Look, I've had a *terrible* day, and I'm tired of getting blamed every time you two screw up!" I plopped the wig back on Robbie's head, collected my pile of stuff off the landing, and finished my proclamation while climbing the stairs. "So...as far as I'm concerned, I know *nothing* of this, I haven't even *seen* you today. I'm going straight to my room, and this conversation never happened. This time, you guys hang alone."

"*C'mon*, Rhonda! We're talkin' a two hundred and fifty buck split!" Richie hollered after me.

I stopped near the top of the stairs and turned with a loud stomp.

"**NO!** Enough! I mean it, Richie! You two better get cleaned up, brush those wigs out, and put all Mom's stuff away **exactly** as you found it before Dad gets home," I turned, continuing up, adding, "or, I'll tell him you bought an *Enquirer*."

"Can we at least use your name then?" Richie begged, not giving up. "Fifty dollars if we use your name? It'll help if they think we're girls."

"**NO, RICHIE!**"

I got to my bedroom door, and while I struggled with the knob I overheard them whispering,

"*Craaaaa-a-bby.*"

"Let's use her name anyway. She'll never know."

"Yeah!"

I slammed the door with my foot, dumped my stuff on the bed, and plopped face-first next to it, spent.

I don't know how much time passed before I finally rolled over, sat up, and took stock of my situation.

I had my room. It was my refuge; not particularly girly, its feminine touches only hinted at by the few remnants of my mother's last makeover attempt, like the now sun-faded lace-edged, powder blue forget-me-not print curtains on my window she put there when I first entered high school.

My high school years had slowly erased her futile feminizing efforts into an office-like appearance: my electric typewriter occupying space on the desk where she had arrayed makeup and perfume bottles, all now relegated to my bathroom cabinet's bottom drawer; a portable TV on the bureau hid an embroidered doily below it; more books than I had shelves for were stacked about; and my prize: a new beige push-button phone, a 16th birthday present from my parents, which I loved, even though it was the "Princess" version with buttons that light, was next to the bed. I had bulletin boards full of test papers, news clippings, and college brochures, an oversized wall calendar pinned up next to my desk with all my days until graduation scheduled out and color-coded, and a sparsely-filled closet of practical, functional clothing. I'd lately gravitated toward wearing nothing but bib overalls, as I found the breast pockets useful for carrying my main pride and joy: a state-of-the-art HP pocket calculator.

I zipped open my gym bag and peeked inside, hoping not to see them.

The cheerleader uniform and pompoms were still there.

I extracted them, placed them in a neat pile on the bed, and examined them like they were rare cultural relics. I felt the form-fitting knit top, and traced a finger around the embroidered letters spelling out "Tigers." I tossed a pompom in the air to watch it expand at its apex and rustle back to the bed. I stood, holding the skirt to my waist, and swung my hips from side to side, eyeing the motion of the tidy pleats.

Is this stuff really every girl's dream? The ultimate symbols of feminine achievement in high school society?

It angered me to admit it, but they did seem to hold an uncanny allure. When one of my peers walked down the hall dressed up in this stuff, I did feel envy rear in me just as it did in everyone else, despite my better judgment.

But, what the heck was this uniform doing here? With *me*?

I reached into my bib pocket and extracted the torn slip of paper. I crossed to the phone, and without looking at it, punched in Bud's phone number from memory.

I hung up before it rang on the other end.

What the heck was I doing calling Bud? What would I even say? Tell him he gave me his phone number because I turned into a cheerleader in some sort of creepy reverse-werewolf transformation? How could I tell him, or *anyone*, about all this nonsense without having them think I'd gone completely bonkers?

I tucked Bud's slip of paper into my empty jewelry box, turned back to the bed, and picked up the pompoms again.

I didn't ask for these, and didn't want them; I didn't want anything to do with this stuff. No, whether this day was real or imagined, whether it was a dream or not, I didn't like what this uniform stood for, or how it mocked me.

Brains were everything to me, and beauty, worthless.

Brains **had** to win. It was a matter of pride. More than that: of life or death. And, in order to win, brains would have to fight back.

Or...at least refuse to play beauty's game.

I stuffed the uniform and pompoms back into my gym bag, resolving to return them to Coach Tarbo tomorrow.

Chapter Seven

BROTHERS FROM ANOTHER PLANET

When Dad announced dinner, I came down to the dining room and sat in my usual place across the oval table from Richie and Robbie. At this moment, the boys were out of their Joan Rivers makeup and being unnervingly well behaved.
Adorable, in fact.

Why was it that our shared red hair and freckles looked so cute, boyish, and irresistibly appealing on my little brothers, whereas, on me, the same basic stuff looked hideous? Boys are lucky that way. At eleven years old, Richie had just begun to evolve into his adult features, and it was becoming pretty obvious he'd be transforming into "ruggedly handsome" any day now. Robbie, eight, still had a good year or two left to exude the pure, impish, big-eyed charm of Opie. He'd evolve to handsome someday too, no doubt.

But...*me?* Hopeless. The best I could ever expect in the looks category was "interesting."

Our red hair came from Mom, but hers, Richie's, and Robbie's was the color of a glowing sunset, shiny-smooth, and picked up highlights of gold where the sun bleached it; none of theirs was the matte, dried-blood red, frizzy rat's nest of mine. Sure, I got Mom's pretty, pale skin, but hers was a freckle-less alabaster and was coupled with striking, jade green eyes, not the indecisive hazel I was born with. Mom couldn't be invisible even if she tried.

Both my brothers tidily placed their napkins on their laps and smiled at me. I knew better than to trust it. Something was up.

Dad came in, carrying a casserole between hot-mitts.

It was obvious he was the one who my two bratty brothers' features would eventually resemble, curse them. Dad was by far the handsomest man I'd ever known and, although his chestnut-brown, wavy hair had a bit of gray at the temples now, he had a deep chin-dimple, like Cary Grant, to help carry off "distinguished" to perfection. I inherited only the mere whispering hint of that chin dimple, and it was by far my favorite physical trait, just about the only thing about my face I really did like. And Dad's neutral face rested into an easy smile, unlike mine; the corners of my mouth turned down when they settled.

Mom was the first to point it out to me. *Thanks, Mom.* She claimed it was probably because some of her distant relatives had been professional mourners, but I was pretty sure she was joking about that part.

I adored Dad. He was really the only person in the world I could talk to about *anything*; Mom definitely wasn't. Fortunately, she had to work most nights, so I resolved right then and there to try to *somehow* tell Dad all about my weird day while I had the chance without Mom interfering and trying to control the conversation.

"Okay, guys," Dad said, seating himself at the head of the table, removing the mitts, and cutting what looked to be Mom's "world famous" lasagna into soft-form squares. "Dig in."

Robbie jumped up and immediately began piling his plate with square after oozy square.

"Dad, may I talk to you about something?" I asked, shifting a wary eye to my brothers and back, wondering if this might not be the best time after all.

"Sure, Ron, wha...*Whoa, Robbie!* Save some for the rest of us!"

"I'm *very* hungry."

Dad stood and scooped one square from Robbie's plate onto Richie's, one to mine, then one to his own, and slid all but one back into the casserole dish.

"You finish this first, and if you're still hungry, you can have seconds," he commanded, then fell into his usual daily recap. "Well kids, your Dad had a busy day today. A full facelift and two rhinoplasties. One of them a man. Heh, it's not just rich matrons and movie stars anymore."

Richie dropped his fork to his plate with a clank and chimed, "Mom says," with Robbie joining him to finish in unison, "keep the surgical table off the dinner table."

"I wasn't going to go into detail," Dad defended.

Not to be derailed, I tried again.

"Dad, I...."

"Robbie, eat your dinner, don't play with it," Dad scolded.

But Robbie had already constructed what appeared to be a lasagna-noodle-version of Devil's Tower by rolling up some of the flat noodles into a cone, all the while in a wild-eyed stare, like he was possessed. This plan to build Devil's Tower must have been his ulterior motive while piling so much food on to his plate, I realized, and I braced myself for whatever brotherly insanity that was to inevitably follow.

"It must be 'cause of what happened today, Dad. It must be 'cause of the aliens," Richie offered.

Here it comes.

"What aliens, Richie?" my father asked, arching an eyebrow.

Richie stood and raised his hands over his head in anticipation of letting loose his whopper de jour. I sighed, slumped back in my chair, knowing I'd just been derailed, and resolved it was a good time to eat.

"I know you're not gonna believe me, Dad, but it's *true*—I swear to *God!*

"Let's leave God out of this nonsense, Richard," Dad scolded.

"It's not nonsense, Dad! Robbie and I were in the back yard just mindin' our own business, and these huge, like, clouds came rolling across the sky, and then there was lightning crashin' all around us, and then everything went black, and then, then...this, like, light beam came down out of a *huge* flying saucer, and a bunch o' these human spongy-lookin' guys with, like, millions of teeth rezzed down and grabbed Robbie, and when I tried to stop them, they, ...they shot me with a stun ray, so I couldn't move, and they rezzed Robbie up into their ship with 'em to study him or something or, or plant an embryo in him...I don't know for sure, because I passed out...but when I came to, they were gone, and Robbie was all covered in ectoplasm, and...!"

On cue, Robbie raised his tee shirt to reveal a tummy covered in raised, red suction-marks.

"See, Dad! Look what the aliens did!"

Dad wore a knowing deadpan.

"I noticed the aliens also left the vacuum cleaner out. Come here, Robbie," Dad urged, examining the round welts. He shook his head at Richie.

"Why do you torture your brother like this?"

"I *knew* you wouldn't believe me, but it's *true*. I *swear*."

"Yeah, yeah...."

"We better tie Robbie up and keep him in isolation until we know he's okay."

Robbie apparently didn't know about this part of Richie's little scenario, and burst from his trance to blurt, "No way!"

"Way!"

And a slap fight ensued.

"**Enough!**" Dad barked, standing, and causing the boys to return sheepishly to their seats. "You'll **both** spend time in isolation. After you finish the dishes, you'll go straight to your room, and **no** TV."

"But tonight's Charlie's Angels," Richie whined.

"Hubba-hubba," Robbie added.

"I said no TV. And I don't want to hear another word about it."

The boys went back to devouring their lasagna, as did Dad, until he finally remembered me, and turned.

"I'm sorry, Ron. What was it you wanted to say?"

I sighed, completely undone. To follow up my brothers' tale with my own even weirder one would be ludicrous. Fortunately, the timer on the VCR and TV on the sideboard at the other end of the table clicked itself on, keeping me from having to answer.

"Don't look, Mom's show started," Richie mock-scolded Robbie, with the hint of a smirk. "*We're* not *allowed* to watch."

The TV displayed the local channel, WTAD's logo, and a super-title reading, "Ask Mom" and there she was, my mother, the celebrity and local-news-call-in-segment-hostess, smiling and waving into the camera from some mock-living room easy chair.

Dad's eyes narrowed at Richie. "You can watch Mom *while you eat*, but that's *all*, Richie."

"How 'bout we trade Mom's show for Charlie's Angels...?"

"Don't push it."

"How do we keep the lines of family communication open in an increasingly technological world?" Mom asked her viewers.

As if she would know.

"Let's go to the phones."

Dad scraped the last bits of lasagna from his plate, finished it off, and rose. He wiped his mouth with his napkin and turned to me.

"I'm off to pick up your mother. Would you mind watching your brothers, and make sure they do what they're told?"

I glanced at Richie and Robbie. Robbie stuck his tongue out at me.

I knew they were in rare form tonight and I would be in for nothing but grief from them, so I had to pick my poison.

I rose, and, clearing Dad's plate along with my own, offered an alternative as I headed for the kitchen.

"I'm all through with my homework. I don't mind picking up Mom tonight."

I glanced back. All three of them stared at the TV, mesmerized, as Mom chattered away.

Dad sat back down without turning, and mumbled, "Sure, hon. If you don't mind."

"Mealtime should be family time," I heard Mom lecture her first caller, "Don't let your kids go out for fast food or eat on their own. Put your foot down. You need to commit yourself to dinner as a family. Make it a requirement—everyone together, no excuses."

It was a surreal, ironic tableau: Mom's voice and image at her end of the table, dominating the conversation as if she was really there.

Chapter Eight

YES, IT'S SUPERMOM

The "ON AIR" light clicked off, but the newsroom was still abuzz with activity when I arrived, so no one noticed me as I stepped over cables, around C-stands, and behind reflectors, heading for the row of small, glassed-in offices against the back wall of the soundstage. I slipped into the one with an incised plastic "Dr. Rosemary Glock" nameplate on its door.

I closed the door soundlessly behind me, and peered out through the window blinds toward my mother. She was bathed in a peach-colored halo of light and having any lingering nose-shine powdered away by Ginger, the make-up girl, before performing her closing segment. The phony living room she sat in, with its squares of alternating blue and green berber carpet, flats of fake bookshelves, and pale, modern birchwood furnishings, gave off an air of cozy sophistication defying the wear-stained concrete floor it sat on.

I rolled the blinds' plastic rod between my fingers, blocking my view of her, but her voice remained, piped in through the studio's sound system.

"Fred, all I'm saying is that if someone calls in with anything that might be considered a working-mother issue," I heard her whisper to her assistant, "Put them through *first*. It's the perfect segue for me to mention my book at the end of the show."

"The station has a policy against on-air product plugs, Rose," Fred reminded.

"But, okay...what if someone calls in and actually mentions my book...? I have to answer *that*, don't I?

And if the best answer is 'It's all covered in the last four chapters' what else *can* I do?"

Fred sighed and mumbled, "I'll have my sister call."

"And make sure my sons don't sneak another call through again. Richie pretending to be a Southern belle trying to teach her kids how to slaughter chickens and having to make a family pet out of her headless mistake: I got nasty letters from the animal rights people for a month."

"No sneaky offspring tonight. Check."

"Live again, Rose," I heard the floor manager call out, "in three, two...."

The polished voice of our local news anchor, Lloyd Cambridge, followed:

"And here again is, 'Ask Mom,' with noted clinical psychologist and author, Dr. Rosemary Glock, where both children and parents are welcome to call in and ask for her special brand of modern, motherly advice. Dr. Rose...?"

"Thank you, Lloyd," Mom replied. "Tonight's continuing topic: family communication. It is the biggest challenge in any parent/child relationship, and the key to a healthy family unit. No matter how busy we are, we parents need to make time for our children, for those we love, time to...."

I slapped the speaker's off switch, dousing the soundproofed office into dead, blissful silence.

I turned to Mom's computer occupying a large part of her desk, its animated screensaver lazily drifting across its screen, and hesitated. She didn't like me "playing" with it, because it was "not a toy," but when was the last time I played with toys? And, the studio had NexisLexis. It was the closest thing to artificial intelligence. You could ask it anything and it knew the answer. And...I already knew how to access it.

I scooted over, sat, and touched a key. The screensaver popped off. In its stead, her prompt sat there on the screen, RG> blinking in green phosphorescence at me, like a startled mouse in front of an antsy cat.

RG, I thought, *those are my initials too*, and I logged on. The modem hummed and beeped its phone numbers, then buzzed and twanged a connection, followed by a shot of static across the screen, then:

LEXIS-NEXIS
THE DATA BANK—NEWS AND INFORMATION SYSTEM

A "search for:" prompt appeared. I thought a moment.

What should I explore tonight?
Of course.

I typed "bites" and hit enter.

A list of file choices appeared: DOG, HUMAN, INSECT, SNAKE, MISC. I typed HUMAN and hit enter.

A massive list of news items scrolled the screen. I further refined my search with "Talbot High, Autumndale," and instantly whittled the list down to a series of vague police reports and news items, *all involving cheerleaders allegedly biting fellow students.*

Wha...?

All at Talbot High? It didn't seem possible, but there was a clear history of enraged cheerleader attacks like mine.

I opened, pored over, and sent each article to Mom's dot-matrix printer. It chirred away at its long feed of folded paper while I accessed and printed more articles, finally reaching the earliest reported incident: a 40-year-old news story involving a girl named Elaine Moody who was expelled for biting another girl in a fit of jealous rage. According to the story, Elaine Moody disappeared before formal charges could be served, and her victim dropped all charges shortly thereafter, without explanation.

I stood and rolled open the blinds just enough to peek through.

Sure enough, Mom sat, holding up her book.

I shook my head and hit the speaker switch.

"...available at bookstores everywhere. And now, here's Ken Cleaver with the weather."

I zipped back to the computer and logged off of the modem, returning the screen to the wandering screensaver.

I dashed over to the printer and refolded my dangling banner of printouts while it continued to whirr away at the final article. When it finished, I tore it free, folded the accordion of pages in two in order to remove the punch strips from both sides at once, tossed the strips into the trash, stuffed the printouts into my book bag, removed my biology text, leafed it open to tomorrow's chapter, and plopped down in Mom's armchair mere seconds before she entered, shadowed by Fred.

"...talk to Fran about lunch tomorrow, pick up the flyers...oh yes, and I'm meeting my agent at four, don't forget that."

Fred wrote it all down into a Filofax, all the while nodding along like a dippy bird.

Mom turned to me.

"How was your day, dear?"

Before I could open my mouth to speak, Mom stole back my airtime.

"It couldn't have been as hectic as mine, but I guess that's what I deserve for agreeing to become 'mother to entire the world.'"

As she continued her prattle, my mind slapped its internal off switch, blocking her out. It wandered elsewhere, as I tried to recall if Wonder Woman ever had a daughter, and if so, whether or not her daughter resented her mother's do-goody fame as much as I resented my own mother's.

Any hope of using the drive home to share my problems with Mom was futile; the time had already been usurped by her show and its callers.

"Even after Fred screens them, it's still a risk putting most of my callers directly on air," Mom chuckled, "Did you hear that women tonight ask me, 'How can I get my new boyfriend to leave his wife?' Or, that *other one?* 'Is it okay if we ask our guests to give us a specific amount of money rather than gifts on our wedding invitations?'

"No, I...."

"But...I suppose I wouldn't have a job without them," she laughed. "My public. And now, with my book...did your father tell you?"

She pulled her Filofax from her side bag and started scribbling, not waiting for my reply. "My agent called today—it's been named a Book of the Month Club Alternate. I'm not sure what that means, but I guess it's good. It was probably just her way of preparing me for the book tour she's planning. I already have local promotional engagements for the next three weekends. Your father's going to *kill* me.

"I'd appreciate your help with your brothers, Rhonda. Please don't let them get too wild when I'm away. Your father's tired when he gets home—he doesn't need the aggravation. Fred's a big help at the office, but so much of this job I simply have to do myself, so I'm counting on you to pitch in at home."

"Sure, Mom," I replied, dutifully.

What else could I say? You can't fight a force of nature, and Dr. Rosemary Glock, PhD was most definitely one of those. I glanced over at her—in her smart suit and no-nonsense wedge-cut hair—simultaneously admiring her and hating her. The hating part was recent; I'd still not completely figured out why.

I opened my mouth to continue, but Hurricane Rosemary turned back and made landfall again.

"Despite all this, I've kept Saturday night free, honey, so we can still have our regular mother/daughter quality time—just us girls. Then I can hear all about your senior year..."

I turned onto our street and started up the block.

"...ah, here we are. What a day. It feels so good to be home. Could you get that box of books in the back for your Mama please, sweetie?"

I parked the car, stomped down the emergency brake and breathed out another, "Sure," as my mother strode up the walk ahead of me.

The front door opened, and she fell into my father's waiting arms. I watched their silhouettes embrace, and yeah, it embarrassed me, but it mostly made me sad, which didn't quite make sense.

Shouldn't I be happy that they still love each other so much?

Then, it hit me: it was because *I* wasn't included in their hug. Mom and Dad had each other. Even Richie and Robbie, they had each other. But, whom did *I* have? Where did *I* fit in?

I sighed, put my book bag on top of Mom's box of books, and waddled into the house.

Chapter Nine

DEEPER DIMORPHIC DILEMMAS

I locked the door to my room before I even thought about it. I usually only locked it before I left for school, to keep my brothers out of my stuff, or when my parents were away, to keep my brothers out of my hair.

This time I must have subconsciously wanted to keep *everyone* out so that I could think.

Thinking didn't help. What is there to think about when nothing makes sense? What I really needed was someone to talk to. A second opinion. Someone to let me know I wasn't crazy.

I hesitated, crossed to my phone, and punched in Bud's number again. It rang once, and then....

"Hello...?"

It was Mrs. Langston's voice.

"Hi, Mrs. Langston, it's Rhonda. Is Bud there...?"

"I think he's been expecting your call," she laughed. "He's been pacing around the house like a caged animal all evening. Just a sec."

I heard a muffled cry, as if Mrs. Langston had one hand over the mouthpiece of the phone as she called out, *"BUD...? TELEPHONE FOR YOU!"*

Expecting my call? That doesn't sound right.

"Hello, Bud Langston here," he crooned, in an overly casual and lower-than-normal voice.

I laughed, and replied, aping his tone, "And, it's Rhonda Glock here...."

"Oh...ah, hi, Ron. Hi," he sputtered, his normal

voice returning, "Um, aah...what's up?"

That's when it hit me: he was hoping for a call from Ronnie.

Oh, brother!

I snorted into the receiver at him. It couldn't be helped. But I couldn't be mad at Bud and talk to him about all this at the same time, so I shook the anger off.

"Hey, listen," I said, lowering my voice to just above a whisper," Are you alone? I need to talk to you about something kinda...*personal*."

"Sure. I'm alone. What's up?"

I swallowed hard and launched in before I could talk myself out of it.

"Well, I uh...I've got this...problem. Anyway, I've got to talk to someone about it, and you're just about the only person I know who I can...trust. It's a little hard to know exactly where to start...You'll probably just think I'm crazy."

Now he laughed, "Ron, you're the sanest person I know."

"You won't think so after I tell you what happened."

There was a pause. I eventually realized it was my pause, not his, and it was because I was holding my breath. I exhaled, took another long breath, and continued.

"Okay, here goes. I...I became a different person today."

He paused, I guess because he was trying to figure out what I meant, then replied, "Oh, well, that's pretty normal for people our age, isn't it?"

"No, Bud, I mean *literally*. I *literally* changed into someone else."

"What...? You mean, like, a religious thing?"

"No, not religious—at least, I don't *think* so.

Look, something really weird is happening to me, and now it's like...I'm two people in one body."

I could hear Bud breathing on the other end, in and out, in and out, as he tried to somehow make sense out of what I was saying.

"A...split-personality...?" he offered, still confused, "like that Eve lady in the movie?

"No. God, this is so embarrassing...the change that happened, it's...*physical*."

There was another pause, more breathing, then Bud whispered, "Don't you think you should be talking to, like...your mother about this?"

"I tried. She's useless."

"Or...ask the school nurse?"

"Nurse Weld? Believe me, she wouldn't believe me."

"Well, what can *I* do?"

"I'm really scared, Bud." I felt my voice crack and I fought back tears. "Now there's this *other person* inside me, and if people find out...."

Bud stopped breathing.

"Oh, God...Rhonda, are you talking about what I *think* you're talking about?"

I reached over, opened my jewelry box, and took Bud's note out. I unfolded it, and pondered.

Could he have somehow figured out Ronnie is me?

"I, I'm...not sure," I responded, "What are *you* talking about?"

"There's...another person? *Inside you?*"

"Um, sure, I guess that's the best way to explain it..."

"Whoa! This is heavy," he wheezed. I heard him trying to catch his breath. He finally came back on the phone and asked, in a hoarse whisper, "Can you tell me...who the *father* is?"

"**FATHER?!** Ugh, no Bud! There's no father, **God!**"

"Well, but...when you said...."

"There's no *guy* involved! Ugh, how could you even think that! I'm not talking about anything like that! See, there's this *girl*...who attacked me...in the locker room. She, well she *bit* me...and I felt...."

"*Yeah...?*"

I suddenly realized where this path was heading and it was even worse than the last one.

"Look Bud, I'm, um...*never mind*. Forget I said anything."

"No, Ron. It's okay," he sighed, sympathetically, "I understand. I have a cousin like that. I'm cool with it."

"No. Bud, I'm not...believe me, that's *not* it!"

I panicked. This phone call had gone completely 180. I needed to bail as quickly as possible.

"Look, forget this whole conversation. Forget everything I said. I gotta go. Bye."

I depressed the hang-up button with a finger so I could bap myself on the head several times with the receiver.

"Stupid," I mewled, between baps, "Stupid. Stupid. Stupid. Now he thinks I'm a lesbo."

I needed something mindless to distract the churning embarrassment, shame, and self-recriminations echoing in my brain. I snapped on my TV and flopped on the bed. A football game in progress bloomed across the screen.

I felt an odd surge of energy across my chest.

With a soft crackle, my breasts began enlarging.

I scrambled off the bed and snapped off the TV.

My breasts deflated.

I hesitated a moment, turned the game back on, and eyed my bust.
It grew.
Off again.
It shrank.
On.
Grew.
Off.
Shrank.
I collapsed on my bed with no other alternative left to me but to sob.

Chapter Ten

HERSTORY

Calculus, biology, and Honors English were not on my priority list the next day at school. Given the enthusiasm I had for academic success, all of my class seats were in the front row. There was no place to hide. My mind kept obsessively repeating humiliating scenarios of what ifs: what if I start to transform during discussions of derivatives; what if my bust begins to bloom during biology; what if my voice changes and I break out in giggles during my recitation of *The Wasteland*? And then there was Coach Tarbo; what would I say to her when I returned Ronnie's uniform?

It wasn't until lunchtime that I realized I had been so distracted at home that morning I had forgotten to pack a meal. I dug through my book bag for any loose change and was surprised by how much I had rattling around in there; more than ample money to afford the school lunch.

I entered the cafeteria and got into line, my brain still fixated on figuring out this Rhonda/Ronnie thing. I felt like one of those supercomputers in sci-fi movies, one that is asked a circular question with no possible answer, and then its mechanical mind whirrs faster and faster and *faster*...until it explodes.

I didn't want my brain to explode, so I tried giving it a break. I inhaled deeply—that did it; I was immediately reminded why I generally chose not to eat in the cafeteria. The smell alone was enough to put me off my lunch. Why was it that, no matter what they were serving in there, it always smelled like boiled cauliflower and cheddar cheese?

I shook off the nasty smell and scanned the cafeteria, deliberately acknowledging my surroundings, trying to engage the rest of my reality instead. Things looked the same as always: the math club guys—why are they always all guys?—were clotted in one corner, comparing pocket calculators, and the loudest group, the drama kids, were in another, comparing egos. The prime tables by the windows were filled by jocks and cheerleaders and, as usual, Bud was among them.

Fortunately, he had his back to me. I turned back to the line, relieved.

"Hey there!"

It was Tanya Sweet, in line, right in front of me, looking straight at me. So I replied, "Hey," only to realize she was actually talking to Felicia Chao, who had stepped into line right behind me.

Felicia then took cuts in front of me to join Tanya without a second thought.

Ah yes, still invisible—forgot for a second.

I was definitely engaging my reality now.

Felicia leaned in conspiratorially toward Tanya.

"*Ohmygawd*, did you hear about *Darleen*?" she only half-whispered, placing a hand over her mouth in melodramatic shock.

"No, do *tell*..." Tanya whispered back, even though—hello!—I was right behind them and could clearly hear every word they said, and I was, after all, the other half of the altercation of topic.

"Her parents are taking her to a shrink today," Felicia explained, drawing circles in the air around her ear with a pink-nail-polished index finger.

Tanya gasped, "*No!*"

"I saw her yesterday," Felicia nodded, continuing. "She looked *hideous*...not like herself at all.

I didn't dare tell her about Ronnie."

"Isn't Ronnie an absolute *doll* though? I didn't mind losing to *her*."

I stepped out of line and hurried out of the cafeteria, feeling slightly nauseated; I wasn't sure if it was caused by the smell in there or the attitude of the pair in front of me, or from having my previous day's nightmare reinvade my reality.

I clipped down the main hallway, hesitating in front of my counselor, Ms. Swanson's, office door.

But...I moved on.

The school psychologist's office was next. I didn't know Mr. Trent. That could be a good thing? He seemed nice. Wasn't this big enough of a problem to seek a professional's advice? But I was pretty sure my particular problem wasn't covered in his area of expertise.

Dammit!

I needed help, and answers, but what could either of them possibly say or do to help me?

Even if they believed me?

I stopped at the center of the rotunda just inside the main entrance. Hallways led off in either direction. Stairways led to the upper floors. Which way was I to go? I was on my own, adrift in uncharted waters, and yeah, *freaked out.* Then I saw it, the school motto, emblazoned above a glass fronted trophy case:

SCIENTIA REGIT,
knowledge rules.

At that moment something clicked in my head: a core belief in my own intelligence. I mean, I was smart, and clever, and resourceful, *wasn't I?* Those assets hadn't failed me yet. In fact, it dawned on me that if I had to choose *anyone* in this whole school, student or faculty member, to help solve a mystery, I'd have to admit *I* was best suited to face just this kind of unique situation.

The scientific method needed to be applied. I already had more than enough questions. It was time to do some research and start finding some answers.

I turned around to head for the library and almost plowed right into Lainey in her custodian's attire. I stopped up short with a gasp. Lainey's eyes widened, then narrowed, as she looked me up and down. She stepped to one side, and continued down the hallway, followed by Dinah, toenails a-clatter on the waxed linoleum floor. With a jangle of keys, they entered her janitor's office/closet through an oddly shaped door with one of its corners lopped off beneath the wedge end of the stairwell. Dinah's milky eyes glanced back at me one last time as the door shut.

The complete collection of Talbot High yearbooks was stored way at the back end of the last row of the school library stacks, on the bottom shelf. I sat on the floor and, pulling the computer print-outs from my book bag, reread the oldest story, scanning it for dates.

I opened the yearbook for 1934, it would be the freshman year of the two girls from the very first biting incident in question: the fight between Elaine Moody and Margaret Boursen. I flipped through and located Elaine's tiny picture. Unfortunately, the freshman pictures were far too tiny to tell me much of anything, so I grabbed the 1935 yearbook.

There was a better picture of Elaine as a sophomore. She looked quite ordinary. Not homely, but fairly plain. Certainly, no beauty. Her hair was straight and she didn't seem to be wearing much, if any makeup. Her interests were all academic, listing "Chemistry Club," "Mathematics Club," "Debate Team," and "Dean's List Honor Student."

Huh. She was a brainy geek, like me.

I flipped the page in search of Margaret Boursen.

She wore a bright smile but was otherwise every bit as plain as Elaine, although not so academic; her only interest listed was, "Glee Club."

I grabbed the next yearbook, 1937. They were both juniors. I flipped through to the junior class pictures, spotting Elaine first, and my breath caught in my throat.

What the...?

Elaine had become *beautiful*. Stunningly and remarkably beautiful, only barely resembling her former self. Here hair was now platinum blond and styled in Fay Wray/Myrna Loy waves, her eyebrows plucked and arched, her lips full and face made up.

Weird.

Okay, I thought, *it happens sometimes*—a girl goes away for a summer and comes back post-puberty hot. Tanya Sweet kinda did that. Well, she was cute already, but over the last summer she grew womanly curves. Estrogen is a powerful hormone, once it kicks in.

I was still waiting for mine to do so.

Elaine's junior-year accomplishments listed, "Most Popular," and "Varsity Cheerleader." Nothing academic to be found.

Hmm. So, what happened to Margaret?

I hurriedly turned the page, giving myself a paper cut. I thrust my finger into my mouth, but not before a small drop of blood eerily landed right on Margaret's picture.

I pulled a tissue from my bag and wiped it off

her face, revealing a still very plain but cheery-looking young woman. It seemed she was a third runner-up for the "Future Homemaker of the Year" award and still in Glee Club.

So, Elaine blossomed in her junior year, while Margaret remained plain. Elaine became popular and Margaret, not.

Interesting.

I pulled 1938: their senior yearbook—and the year of the incident.

Elaine's picture spot was a blank gray square with "No Picture Available" printed in it. The article in my print-out had reported that Elaine vanished after the biting incident so the class pictures must have been taken after that.

I slowly turned the page, found Margaret, and gasped.

Amazing.

In one short year Margaret had now evolved into a true beauty: hair, makeup, the whole nine yards. And, now, among her accomplishments, "Varsity Cheerleader."

"Hey there!" a voice came out of nowhere.

I jumped.

It was Bud, staring over my shoulder. I snapped closed the yearbook, quickly re-shelved all of them, stuffed the print-outs into my bag, and stood.

"Sorry, Ron…didn't mean to startle you," Bud whispered. "I'm glad I finally found you. I've been looking all over. I was worried you, uh, might not be at school today, you know…after your phone call last night."

He glanced away. I could tell he was uncomfortable talking to me.

Great.

"Anyway, I don't want to lose you as my tutor... or my friend," he added. "I asked Ms. Peele if she'd seen you and she told me you went back here in the stacks."

I suddenly realized I'd completely forgotten to meet him in the tutorial center. I glanced at my watch. The lunch hour was nearly over.

Shoot.

"I-I'm sorry, Bud. I flaked out on our session," I stammered, lofting my book bag and heading toward the front desk. I whispered, "Look, about my phone call last night. I was just...." I tried to think of a plausible explanation for my state the night before. "I was upset about a fight I had...with...this other girl. It's really no big deal."

I smiled at him as sincerely as I could fake, but I've never been a very good liar. He eyed me back, and obviously wasn't buying it. It was as if he could see my imaginary self, who was busy chewing on her hair in nervous anguish.

"Right," he nodded. "Well, if you *do* ever want to talk about it, I'm willing."

I let the offer dangle, unanswered.

He got the hint and changed the subject.

"*Right*. Anyway, we still need to organize our lab notes before tomorrow. Can we meet up this afternoon? Say, right after practice?"

"Sure."

"Great, I'll drop by your house, okay?"

"Um...yeah, no problem. I'll see you then."

As we started to leave, I stopped at a table near the library entrance to reorganize my book bag. Bud lingered with me, but then, not knowing what else to say, he backed away and turned.

He stopped at the doors, thought a moment, and returned.

"Hey Ron, you wouldn't happen to know that new girl, Ronnie, would you?"

"Yes. You might even say we're joined at the hip," I grumbled.

"*Really?!* Oh. Well…I was looking for her too. You haven't seen her around today, have you?"

"No, I can honestly say I've not seen her at all today."

Durk then burst through the double doors like they were an opposing team's line and stomped over to Bud.

"Langston, what the hell are you doing in here again? Ronnie wouldn't be hangin' around with these geeks."

Ms. Peele, shushed him from behind her front desk.

Bud jammed his hands into his pants pockets. "I, uh, checked everywhere else," Bud lied, in a whisper. I could always tell when Bud lied because he'd shove his hands into his pockets first. "Did you have any luck?" he asked Durk.

"Nah, she wasn't in the girl's locker room."

"Girls lock…? How do you know that?" Bud smirked.

"Trade secret," he leered back.

"He wears a dress," I whispered loudly enough for both Bud and Ms. Peele to hear.

Ms. Peele snorted, suppressing a spontaneous chuckle.

Durk shot me a scowl, and I grinned back, savoring the small victory of forcing my visibility on him again.

"Maybe she's not here today," Bud suggested.

"She's gonna have to be at the *rally*."

"*Rally?* What rally?" I asked.

"Of course," Bud nodded, "the *rally*."

"Uh, what rally?" I repeated, but wouldn't you know, I'd become invisible again.

"We'll nab her at the door," Durk proposed.

"I'll nab her. You'll watch," Bud shot back, as the two headed for the double doors.

"I haven't seen your brand on her butt yet."

Ms. Peele shushed Durk again, even though he was already half-out the door.

I rushed to the bulletin board between the restrooms to check the school's daily schedule posted there, and ran a finger down it. Just as my finger reached "All School Rally 1:00 PM" my fingernail began to lengthen.

I dashed into the girl's restroom, and locked the door.

I must have been making an awful racket while transforming, because I heard pounding on the door, and Ms. Peele's voice asking if I was okay, and demanding I open the door.

Ronnie opened it instead, all decked out in her cheerleading uniform.

A confused Ms. Peele gave a glance inside the empty restroom looking for me, before turning back to Ronnie.

"Time to rally, Ms. Peele!" Ronnie giggled, as she dashed out.

And I was once again a passenger on Rocket Ronnie, hurling full-bore toward Planet Cute.

Chapter Eleven

ON/OFF SWITCH

Ronnie giggled as we huddled inside a large, fake bass drum, feeling the wheels under us lup-lup-lup across the boards of the gym floor. The slightly muffled sound of the marching band's drumline rat-a-tatted out a fanfare. I watched shadows of hands holding bass drum mallets play across the large pieces of butcher paper hiding us as they pretended to beat against the paper from the outside.

As the drumline rolled a crescendo to a climax, Ronnie exploded from the front of the fake drum to a chorus of *oohs* and *aahs* from the bleachers. The band instantly struck up our fight song as the other cheerleaders pony-hopped in from both sides, and, since Ronnie seemed to know exactly what to do, I remained as passive as possible so as not to inadvertently cause her to trip up.

As their last rally routine, "Kill the Groundhogs," wound down, each cheerleader did a final gymnastic run across the front of the bleachers to end with a flourish and shout her name. I watched from my front row seat inside Ronnie's head as she awaited her turn. The bleachers were full of all my schoolmates: I could see Brenda Kerwin and Eric Polk, predictably ducking under the bleachers to neck. And, true to form, Fred, Ned, and Ted, charter and sole members of the Geekster Club, were third row, center. These proto-electrical engineers wore baseball caps, each topped by a pair of Nixie tubes wired to battery packs and controllers in their laps. The Geekster's numerically displayed scores in bright neon numbers on a scale from one to ten atop their hats for each cheerleader as they finished their turn at roll call.

A small, disheveled clot of dopers slipped out the side door while the principal's back was turned.

Bud and the rest of the team were lined up on the bench in the front row, and catching Bud smiling at me was enough for me to distract Ronnie, which made her drop a pompom. She recovered with enough grace to make it almost seem like an intentional part of the cheer, as it led right into her series of cartwheels and handsprings and an airborne, "Ronnie!" I forced her to glance at the Geeksters afterward to confirm my hypothesis: all three gave her brightly flashing 10s.

Ronnie pony-stepped us off to our seat on the front bench to the left as Coach Ferguson and the team rose and lined up, to cheers from the student body. Coach was handed a mike in order to give his standard speech about team spirit, then school spirit, then praise the team, and then finally, the entire student body, with time-worn platitudes. While my own mind smirked at how badly Coach Ferguson's curly toupee matched his real hair color, and at how odd it was that this tough-guy with his overly-masculine physique who had actually been an Olympic weightlifter was so nervous while speaking in front of all of us kids that his voice trembled, I simultaneously experienced the euphoric emotional rush of Ronnie's earnest excitement as she hung on his every trite word, as if Coach's speech was as profound as hearing Albert Einstein explain general relativity for the first time.

When Coach said, "...school spirit *is* as school spirit *does*...", Ronnie leaned over to Felicia and breathlessly whispered, "That is *sooo* true."

What the hell am I doing here?

Before I had time to complain too much, his speech ended and we bounced in a synchronized row out the door to the band playing the school fight song again, followed by the football team and their coaches.

Once out the door, Bud and Durk quickly worked their way past the others and up to me.

"Ronnie! Wait up!" Bud called, waving a hand above the fray.

Ronnie stopped and spun to face them.

"Oh, hi, Bud! Hey, Durk!" she perked.

"Hi," Durk and Bud replied together. There was a bit of an awkward lull. I used it to study their faces. Both looked frozen in a combination of fear and awe. Bud moved first, by inhaling, but Durk, being a natural competitor, used his reserve air to speak first.

"Ronnie," he blurted, then inhaled in a gasp to continue, "since, like...you're new here, I thought that maybe I could, you know...show you around. Introduce you to the right people...you know?"

Bud opened his mouth to interrupt, but Durk jabbed an elbow into his pal's ribs.

"Anyway, I'm havin' a party at my place Saturday night. There'll be beer! Wanna come?" Durk finished up by leaning closer and flashing his puppy-dog grin.

"I can't, I'm busy Saturday, sorry," Ronnie answered, much to my surprise.

Wait a minute. What does she have planned that I don't know about?

I felt someone over my right shoulder and I pivoted to see Durk's current girlfriend, Lydia Markham, had walked back to join us. She looked right at Durk, narrowed her eyes, glanced askance at Ronnie, then shot a knowing look back at Durk.

"Cute, isn't she?" Lydia commented to Durk. She took his arm in hers and pulled him away as he suddenly pretended, a little bit too late, not to notice Ronnie.

"Yeah. I mean, no...um, *who* are you talkin' about?"

Ronnie turned to face Bud, who was still working hard to find his voice.

"He's funny," Ronnie giggled.

"Durk's kind of a jerk, to be honest," Bud whispered, with a chuckle.

Bud's demeanor deflated a bit.

"What's wrong?" Ronnie asked.

"Well," Bud confessed, "I was gonna ask you if you wanted to go out with *me* Saturday night, but I guess you're already busy, huh?"

"I'm not busy," Ronnie replied, confusing both Bud and me.

"Oh, uh...you're not?" Bud stammered. "Then...does that mean you could go out with me?"

I don't know if Ronnie was feeling my confusion or it was her own, but she answered, "Maybe. *I'm not sure.* Anyway, I have to change now. Bye."

I could feel my breasts already beginning to shrink as Ronnie dashed to the locker room with Bud still in pursuit.

"*Wait!* Ronnie, I...."

As I ducked in through the girl's locker room door with Bud still on my heels, he ran right into Coach Tarbo on her way out.

"I think you've got the wrong door, buster," I heard her say before I ducked into an empty toilet stall.

Once free of Ronnie and back to normal, I cut AP English and returned to the library. Ms. Peele led me to the door marked "Archives" and opened it for me.

"Thanks, Ms. Peele."

"Just push in the lock button from the inside and pull it shut when you're done," she explained as she stuffed her wad of keys back in her smock and returned to the front desk.

I looked inside the dim room. The door's sign had oversold it; it was a broom closet with some portable metal racks along three walls, a desk equipped for book repair, and a high, very tiny window for light. A single bare bulb hung from the ceiling. I pulled its chain, sending shadows dancing about as it swung into a final settle, then I turned to close the door behind me.

I scanned the shelves and soon spotted what I was after: cardboard boxes marked "Talbot Tribunes" stuffed in a dusty corner of a lower shelf. Aiming for the oldest ones meant lifting the more current boxes out of the way first. When the age-dried cardboard felt like it might crumble under its own weight, I knew I was close.

And suddenly, there it was: "Student Expelled Over Biting Incident." And beneath that headline was a picture of a homely girl with the full story. The caption under the picture named her as Elaine Moody. I slipped out of the archive back to the stacks for the old yearbook again. The last picture of Elaine Moody, from her junior year, was of a remarkably beautiful girl.

Weird.

I took both the paper and yearbook to the Xerox machine and dug enough change from my daypack to make copies of both the article and the yearbook page.

I returned to the archive and put everything back as I found it, turned out the light and locked the door behind me.

I didn't want to go into class late; I'd have

to explain my tardiness somehow and I was far too distracted to come up with any plausible excuse at the moment, so I resolved to cut it. I sat in my usual spot on the back steps of the science building instead, studying the two pictures of Elaine Moody again. It hardly seemed possible that they were the same person. But no one would ever guess that Ronnie and I were the same person either. There *had* to be a connection. I looked at the homelier one more closely. There was something about it, like I had seen her face somewhere before. But *where?*

Across the schoolyard, the creak of unoiled rollers distracted me. It was Lainey, pushing her cleaning cart into the main building, followed by Dinah.

I shivered.

So creepy. Especially that dog's eyes.

Whatever, I thought and returned to further scrutinize the photos.

That's weird.

Elaine's sweater had an "L" embroidered on it, not an "E"...could it be...?

Elaine? Lainey?

The...janitor?

I grabbed up my books and notes and sped off into the main building. Inside, there was no sign of her. She and her dog had magically vanished again.

A few hallways later I ended my search for her at her funny-shaped little custodial closet door under the stairwell in the rotunda.

I hesitated, then knocked.

Of course, I immediately regretted doing so and was about to dash off when the door creaked ajar and Lainey's face peeked out.

"Oh, it's you." The door opened further and she stepped out, furrowing her already heavily-creased brow, and straightening up.

I hadn't realized how large Lainey actually was, due to her normal stooped posture.

I stepped back.

That's when I noticed she held a single yellow rose in one gnarled hand.

Dinah waddled out from behind the door and stood between her bowed legs. The creepy little dog stared up at me again though her milky eyes, making me take another step back.

A knowing smile curled Lainey's lips.

"Ah. I wondered which one of you girls would show up," she said. She looked me up and down and added, "You seem brighter than the rest of them. What's your name, dearie?"

"Rhonda Glock. And you're...*Elaine Moody*," I responded pointedly.

She nodded. "Oh, you're a smart one all right."

Dinah padded over to strop my leg and let out what sounded just like a soft mew followed by a purr.

"In the house now, Dinah. There's a girl," Lainey cackled. Dinah obeyed. Lainey looked back at me. "I wanted a cat, but I'm allergic. Dinah humors me. She likes you. She doesn't like many people."

Lainey opened the door wide, stepping to one side. I remained frozen.

"Wouldn't you like to come in and chat?"

Lainey backed further into the doorway and with the gesture of an arthritic hand, beckoned me to follow. My mind flashed to the story of Hansel & Gretel, and then the realization that I'd not left a single breadcrumb for anyone to follow. I hesitated.

"Don't be afraid. Just us girls."

What the heck.

I knew I couldn't stop now, just as I was about

to find some real answers. I swallowed my fears and followed her into the small custodial closet, pulling the door closed behind me.

Although appearing to be quite small from the outside, her closet actually opened up into a continuation of the wide, main stairwell above it, which spiraled down another level to the basement. A warm light rose from below. Where I would have expected a subterranean chill and the smell of musty dampness, I was met with cozy warmth and the aroma of freshly-baked cookies.

I stopped at the base of the stairs to take it all in. The vast poured-concrete basement level opened up to a ceiling enmeshed in a sculptural tangle of pipes and valves, some branching from a monstrous glowing boiler, others from a water main, and more intersecting and enlarging back to a massive sewer drainage pipe heading out through the wall in the direction of the street. There were many rows of storage shelves stretching off into darkness, stuffed with everything left over from the birth of the building on: paint cans, tools, old stage props, film projectors, old office supplies, with boxes of every shape and kind stuffed between and on top of them. The silhouettes and shadows of stacks and piles of broken desks, chalk boards, room dividers and such angled about on the right.

To the left, Lainey had arranged a tidy and comfortable sitting room: an overstuffed couch with velvet pillows atop a large, oval rag rug. Dinah was already curled up atop one of the pillows. There was a recliner covered in wide wale corduroy and a coffee table in front of the couch. A linoleum-topped counter with a toaster-oven, hotplate, and sink ran along the nearby wall.

Its conceptual similarity to my mother's stage

set made me uneasy; the incongruity of something that appears to be something else, like an elaborately constructed lie, made me not trust either setting.

Lainey crossed to the sink to trim the stem of her rose. She took a small crystal bud vase from a shelf and, filling it with water, placed the rose in it. She carried it to the center of a 1950's style chrome and turquoise Formica dinette set where there lay a plate of chocolate chip cookies—obviously the source of the cookie aroma—and a steaming pot of brewing tea, set out for two.

She knew I was coming?

Lainey turned and asked me, "So what do you want to know first: who, what, where, when, why, or how?"

"I...I don't understand," I replied, as I cautiously inched toward the table.

"Oh, you understand a lot more than you pretend, a smart girl like you. After all, you're the first one to connect it to me, so you already discovered the 'who.' Me. *I did it*. I invented the spell when I was even younger than you. You're not the only smart one, you know."

Lainey sat and poured out, filling my cup first, and I sat down across from her, my eyes never leaving her face.

"But...."

"Why?" She laughed. "Because I could. There have been, let's just say, powers in my family for centuries."

Lainey took her eyes from mine and looked over to my pile of books.

"Let me see it." She demanded.

"See what?"

"The Xerox copy of my old yearbook picture.

Dinah saw you make it."

I glanced over to the ancient Chihuahua, now curled up asleep on the sofa cushion.

I rummaged through my daypack, found the Xerox and handed it to Lainey. She flattened out the folds and spun it to face me, pointing a gnarled index finger at a square-jawed boy on the same page.

"It's because of him; he's the reason this whole business started. Bart. I wanted Bart. He was a football star, like your friend, Bud." Her eyes misted up. "Bart was beautiful. He deserved someone beautiful. But... well, *I* wasn't beautiful, was I?"

She offered me a chocolate chip cookie. I took it and bit into it, its aroma made it impossible to do anything else. The chocolate was still soft, a warm liquid inside a crisp exterior, and to have something so delicious and familiar calmed me, even as I fretted, looking at Lainey and hearing her story, that I might be seeing my own future self.

"So...I wrote a spell," Lainey continued. "Like I told you, I was smart. I researched the generations of mystical spells amassed by my ancestors and concocted the perfect elixir and incantation. It was exquisitely specific and just the thing to attract the captain of the football team. It made me both irresistible to him and the most beautiful cheerleader in the school."

She picked the rose from the bud vase to admire and sniff it.

"And, unlike this rose, my spell was powerful enough for my beauty not to fade, but to go on and on. No, it was designed to be permanent, or so I *thought*."

She looked at the Xerox again and sighed.

"And it got me Bart. It did," she smiled. "We commanded everyone's attention. We were an unstoppable team. We even planned to marry once we graduated. Everything was perfect, until one day—it was a trivial thing—there was one rather insignificant girl of no particular intelligence or beauty who smiled at Bart. Bart smiled back."

"Margaret Boursen?" I interjected.

Lainey nodded.

"Looking back on it, he was probably only being polite, but it frightened me, enough to threaten me, and...to outrage me. So, I shoved the girl and called her a flirt. She laughed at me and told me I was being silly; well, I suppose I was, but I was also greedy and selfish and very powerful and very, very angry. Nobody was going to laugh at me."

I watched as the rose in her hand withered. She placed it back in the vase.

"Ah, well. I was still so very young."

She sipped the last of her tea and studied the leaves in the bottom of her cup.

"Damn," she muttered, setting it down.

"Anyway, I flew into a rage and in the midst of our fight, I *bit* her."

She looked me square in the eyes.

"Rage and love are the two strongest conductors of metaphysical power in the universe. In that one bite, all the power of my spell flowed out of me and into her. My beauty faded. Hers bloomed. And, true to my spell, Bart had to fall in love with her instead of me. My punishment was...to be left alone again and even uglier than before."

I set down my cup, half finished.

This is crazy. Magic. Spells? I don't believe this voodoo, but what else makes any sense?

I looked at the rose I had just seen dry up before my eyes. How could that be explained, except by magic? I took another sip of tea, and looked at Lainey. There she sat, still staring at the Xerox of her love, Bart, a tear welling in the corner of her eye.

I felt sorry for Lainey, it was hard not to, but only, well...*kind of* sorry for her. After all, she created this monster of a spell that, through no fault of my own, had now befallen me. I needed more answers, so, even though she made me nervous, I took a deep breath, took my last gulp of tea, set the cup down, and pressed further.

"But I don't understand, Lainey. I only change some of the time, not all the time."

"My old spell's been bouncing around this school for years, like a spark from a fire, losing power each time it transfers."

Well...how do I get rid of it? There must be a way to undo it? Right? What can I do?"

She thought for a moment.

"Bite someone?" she cackled, seeing only dark comedy in my situation, which made me mad, and I almost contemplated biting *her*.

"Will that change me back?" I asked. "Will it make me normal again?"

Lainey stopped laughing and shook her head.

"No, you would only end up wearing the ugliness of that action for the rest of your life," she said, more to herself than to me.

"Can't *you* do something?" I cried. "Can't *you* fix it? I mean, dammit, it's *your* spell, right? You must know *some* way to undo it!"

Lainey bristled and I realized only after I'd raised my voice to her that I'd overstepped. She rose and leaned in across the table, putting her face right in mine.

"Why?" she snarled. "Most people think beauty is a gift from God. Nobody wants to be ugly. Get used to it. You might actually like it."

Dinah hissed at me from across the room.

"But, but..." I sputtered back, trying to be brave despite my fear of her, "I *don't* like it. It's not *me*."

"Well who the hell are *you*?" she sneered.

Then, Lainey's eye caught my empty teacup. She picked it up, examining the leaves in its bottom.

I grabbed the Xerox and stuffed it back in my daypack. Lainey held my cup up closer to the light and rotated it a bit. Her face softened.

"Let me...think on this," she muttered in a softer tone, "If I come up with anything to help, I'll let you know. Until then, you're on your own."

"Well, **thank you**," I snipped, with an edge of sarcasm in it, still scared, but also mad, still stinging from her rebuke. I headed to the stairwell, paused, relented with a sigh, and turned back. "I'm sorry. Thank you, Lainey," I repeated, sincerely this time. "And...thank you for the tea."

Chapter Twelve

THE UGLY TRUTH

"Who the hell are *you*?"
Lainey's rebuke stung, because it could have so easily come from me, to myself. The question repeatedly posed itself as I headed out to the student parking lot on my way home. I assume it is a question every young person asks themselves when they approach adulthood, right? And my truth-seeking mind, coupled with my general defensiveness, demanded that I answer myself honestly: *I'm a smart kid,* I admitted, *full of potential—in love with someone beyond my reach. I'm a person who tries to be fair and honest and kind. Who wants to be loved back. But, I'm invisible.*

Then suddenly, I remembered and checked my watch.

Oh, no! Bud's coming over to my house to do our lab notes!

I broke into a run for the family station wagon, which was parked right next to Eric Simon's Pontiac Le Mans. Eric was one of the few boys in school who owned his own car, so he made a point to polish it after school—a lot. He was doing so as I mumbled a quick, "'Lo," and dug out my keys.

He nodded back as he buffed and eyed me. Eric had been seated next to me in trig last semester. I guess I wasn't completely invisible to him. He'd actually talked to me a couple of times, and I'd caught him periodically glancing my way in class, but I wasn't really sure if it had been me or my test answers he was interested in, to be honest. Other kids didn't really like him—he was kind of a know-it-all and his conversational manner was blunt—but then that's what everyone probably thought of me too.

"How goes it, Rhonda?"

I pried open the driver's-side door and heaved my overfilled daypack across to the passenger's seat with a grunt.

"Uh, fine. I guess. A little overloaded with schoolwork today. Gotta run."

Eric came around the front of his car and approached, with the open car door between us while spinning his polishing rag in the air like pizza dough. He gripped the door, preventing me from shutting it just yet.

"Hey, I was thinkin'. You don't go to the school dances much. In fact, I don't think I've ever seen you at one, and well...I'm thinkin' you might wanna go."

I didn't know how to react, so I stood mute and wondered what my face might be saying to him without my meaning it to.

"So...would you want to go to a dance sometime? *With me?* There's one this Saturday night."

"You're...asking me to the dance?" I replied, glancing at my watch again.

"Sure. Why not?"

He smiled at me. He was a good student and actually not bad looking. I felt uncomfortable gooseflesh starting and crossed my arms.

"We could have a really good time together, you know? I like girls like you."

"Girls like *me*...?"

"Sure. With girls like you, there's no bullshit. I mean, you get to go to the dance and I get what I want. We *both* get what we want. You know?"

"I see."

I flashed a tight smile back, got in the car and pulled the door closed, punching down the lock. I started the engine. Eric stepped back and tapped on the window.

"Whadda ya say?"

I backed out of my space and paused. He approached the window again, shrugging.

I flipped him off, and headed home.

When I entered the front door, I called out for my brothers.

"Richie? Robbie? I'm...home...?"

There was silence. This did not bode well. I scanned the foyer.

Okay, no obvious booby traps or anything.

I turned toward the living room only to see Richie and Robbie's clothes lying on the living room floor, empty, but with shirts tucked in pants, socks in shoes, posed out as if they had fallen down dead, and their bodies had disappeared, leaving only an outline of what looked to be fireplace ashes spread wherever their bodies should have been.

Riiight.

I snorted, threw my daypack on the landing and pulled the vacuum cleaner from the front hall closet. I plugged it in, kicking their clothes aside as I began sucking up the ash.

At the sound of the vacuum, my brothers emerged from behind the living room couch dressed in nothing but their underpants.

"What if that had really been us?" Robbie asked, looking at me as though he was about to cry. Robbie was an excellent little actor, but I had already learned not to let his emotional blackmail get to me, the way it so easily manipulated Mom and Dad.

"You'd better hope this comes out of the carpet or you guys'll be a lot worse off than this," I groused, pointing to what was left of their ashy display.

I momentarily turned off the vacuum and looked at him. Robbie had even managed to make a real tear rolled down his cheek.

This kid is good.

But I still wasn't buying it.

"Robbie!" I snapped, startling him out of his act, "Go get the rug shampoo and some rags. Now! And *you...*" I turned to Richie and kicked their clothes into a pile while starting up the vacuum again, "Laundry!"

Knowing I meant business, Richie gathered the clothes and both he and Robbie scurried off.

"And for God's sake, *put some clothes on!*"

I got the last of the ashes up and was rubbing the freshly-shampooed patch of carpet with a dry towel when the doorbell rang. I tossed the towel on the floor of the front closet, took a deep breath, and ran my hands through my hair before opening the door.

It was Bud.

I smiled sweetly, trying to look as calm as I could.

"Hey! Come on in," I chirped.

Bud entered. He looked at me with a quizzical smile. He stepped closer, reached out, and touched my nose with an index finger, then held it up.

"I didn't know it was Ash Wednesday," he smirked.

"Wha...?"

I crossed to the foyer mirror and rubbed the rest of the ash smudge off my nose with a tissue. What could I do? I laughed and pointed to the floor.

"The rug rats disintegrated on the carpet."

"For real, I hope."

"No such luck," I replied, motioning with my head as Richie and Robbie entered, now fully clothed, thank God.

"Hey, guys," Bud chuckled.

My brothers looked Bud up and down, then at each other, then back at Bud.

"You still into sports?" Richie asked, cocking his head to one side.

"Yup."

"Make a muscle," Robbie demanded.

Bud laughed, knelt, bared his bicep, and flexed.

The fantasy me swooned as the real me rested a hand on the hall table to assure my stability.

Robbie poked at it. He turned to Richie and they nodded in agreement.

"Steroid abuse."

The boys headed up the stairs.

Bud stood, laughing, and turned to me.

"How'd *you* end up so normal?"

If he only knew.

"C'mon," I replied, motioning toward the living room, "we can work in here."

As Bud and I sat on the couch side by side, compiling and consolidating our lab notes, the other events of my day faded: Lainey, my brothers' antics, Eric's blunt quid pro quo offer, and even the existence of Ronnie. It felt as if the fantasy me had just taken over completely in the same way Ronnie did. I could sense I was losing control of my emotions and becoming more receptive to my rash romantic feelings toward Bud, but it all felt so natural to be sitting here, side by side with him—so easy, so comforting and comfortable. It felt like we were little kids again, playmates, building Lincoln

Log houses and playing board games, or making mud pies in the yard.

Is this what true love feels like?

"Here's the stuff on sponges," Bud said, handing me his now-tidily re-scribed stack of notes.

I took the three-hole-punch and, feeding the papers in, gave it a whack. One of the little round paper plugs popped out of the punch and fluttered down to land on his thigh. While Bud scanned his notebook for anything else he missed, I reached over to pluck it off and felt goosebumps go down my back. He kept his head bowed and didn't seem to be bothered by my touch.

I continued eyeing him. I'd always loved the way his hair tapered to the center so neatly at the back of his neck, and his small, perfectly shaped ears that lay close to his head. Now, with his strong, man-sized neck and broad shoulders, I had an overwhelming urge to run my hands over them.

I tried to shake off the urge and forced my brain to think about other things, which made me think of Ronnie, which then made me think about Bud's infatuation with *her*. Which then made me mad.

Damn. I'm my own rival!

"So," I asked, now curious to dig deeper into this fresh thought, "did you ever find Ronnie?"

Bud turned to me and lit up with a grin.

"She was at the rally—weren't you there? Man! She was unreal. She's gotta be the best cheerleader Talbot's ever had."

Embarrassed by his own enthusiasm, he quickly dropped his eyes to stare at the floor and I watched those perfect ears of his blush pink.

"Of course," he admitted, "I'm a little biased. But I think she likes me too, Ron."

"And...*you* like *her*."

"Of course," he answered, looking to me as if it should be obvious. "Why? Don't you?'

"I...really haven't quite decided *what* I think of her yet," I replied truthfully. "In some ways...she makes me feel good."

"Right! I know, huh!"

He looked me straight in the eyes, grinning. "I asked her to go out with me this Saturday night, you know. After the game," he confessed.

"*Really?* And what did she say?"

"She's not sure if she can go yet, I guess. She probably has to check with her parents. With a daughter like that, her folks probably built a brick wall around her."

"Undoubtedly," I smirked, recalling how little interest in my romantic life my parents had ever expressed.

"Anyway, she said she'd call me."

"Oh," I answered, with more of an edge to my voice than I'd planned.

I couldn't help it; it *really* irked me. He was all hot on Ronnie and he really didn't know the first thing about her. Only that she was pretty. And I've been here right next to him most of our lives, and...well, what did he think of *me*? Or did he even think of me at all? I might regret it but I needed to know if I was as invisible to him as I was to everyone else, so I pressed.

"Maybe she's waiting to be asked by someone else," I offered, sounding as casual as possible.

"No way. Durk asked her, and she gave him empty air."

"So, she's not a *complete* idiot."

"It's really frying me out, having to wait for an answer."

"So, were you gonna take her to the dance?"

"The dance? Nobody goes to the dances."

"I don't know. I always thought it'd be kinda fun."

"Nah, I'm gonna take her to Durk's party. I wish I could get a definite answer."

"Seems kinda silly to wait. Why don't you ask someone else instead?"

Nope. Gonna wait. She's the only one I wanna go with."

"Oh."

My "Oh" *definitely* came out clipped and I knew the minute it left my lips Bud would see right through me. There was an uncomfortable lull in the conversation. Bud rubbed the back of his neck, then hit the nail right on the head.

"Ron, do you want *me* to ask *you* out?"

I feigned incredulity.

"Wha...**what** in the world are you talking about?"

He looked at me and it was clear he wasn't buying my act. I could feel myself blush.

"I, I'm kinda confused here," he stammered. "What about your...gender issues?"

"My **what!**" I blurted, and stood. "Look, Bud. *I am not a lesbian*, if that is what you are thinking. *God!* Can we just...stop this whole conversation *right now?!*"

"Wait, wait, wait a sec," he said, standing and taking my hands in his. "I have to say this, Ron, because...you're my friend. My best friend. You can always tell me *anything*. You're like a *sister*..."

I pulled free and went into a full rant, stomping about the room as I spoke—it couldn't be helped.

"Okay, then I'm telling you to sit back down and finish our bibliography, *brother!* You think I care about going to a dumb dance? For your information, someone else already asked me to it today and I said no, so I don't know what you're talking about! I was talking about you and Ronnie, but if you're too sensitive and all, then let's just drop it!"

Bud slumped back onto the couch, rubbing hard at the back of his neck again.

"I was just trying to explain how I feel...*about you*," he sighed.

"So, now I know. I'm your *sister*," I snapped, returning to the coffee table to put things away. "Look," I continued, "let's call it quits for tonight, there's other stuff I need to do before my folks get home."

"Sure," he muttered, as he quickly repacked his bag and stood. He headed to the door and, without turning back, said, "See you in class. And, uh, thanks."

The door clicked closed. I stuffed everything else into my daypack, bolted up the stairs and into my room, locked the door, dropped my pack, and fell on my bed.

Chapter Thirteen

REMOTE CONTROL

I reached for another tissue from the bedside table without looking up, but the box was empty. I sat up.

I found myself in the middle of a crater of used tissues. I plucked out one that looked to still have some use in it and wiped my nose dry.

Damn.

I wasn't usually a crier. I never saw much point in it. I blamed this current tendency to do so on Ronnie and the spell.

It must be messing with my hormones.

I inhaled a staccato breath and sighed. But... what else could I do but cry? There seemed no logical, rational solution to my problem. In frustration, I tossed the wet wad of tissue across the room. It missed the trash can and bounced off of one of my posters— the one that said, "When life gives you lemons, make lemonade." It had a cartoon of a guy with a funnel in his head collecting a shower of lemons. His nose was a spigot, pouring lemonade into a pitcher, and he wore a sandwich board advertising his lemonade for two cents a glass.

The thought isn't even worth that.

But...it actually got me thinking.

What if...there's a way to control this thing, to control Ronnie? Maybe there's a way I can at least make this thing work for me until I can find a way to get rid of her. But...how?

I reran everything that had happened to me

so far though my head to analyze it for any possible weaknesses.

Then it hit me.

I bolted down the stairs to the kitchen table. The daily paper was still there. I flipped through to the TV listings and scanned, then ripped it out to take with me.

Perfect.

I bolted back to my room, locked the door, and dug around in my desk for my Walkman and a fresh cassette tape. Tossing them on the bed, I turned on my TV, clicking channels around until I found it: a Saints-Cardinals game. As the TV snow cleared to show players prancing and smashing about on the field, my breasts immediately began to expand. I click the TV off, slipped into my bathroom, stuffed some cotton balls into my ears, set my Walkman next to the speaker, hit record and, donning sunglasses, turned the game back on.

The cotton balls and sun glasses didn't work, and in a matter of moments I was giggling away as Ronnie, with no idea what she would do now.

Damn.

She pulled the cotton from her ears and crossed to the phone. Removing the sunglasses, she chewed on one of their ear rests as she dialed. Apparently, she had access to my memory banks because I watched her dial Bud's home number from heart.

Double-damn.

I heard his mother answer, but then Bud must have wrested the phone away before Ronnie said, "Hello?"

"Hello?" Bud replied.
"Is that you, Bud?"
"Yes, it is. Is this...*Ronnie?*"
"It is! Hi, Bud!"

"Hi."

Ronnie giggled and Bud laughed like a fool on the other end and my reaction to the whole thing was so strong I was actually able to roll Ronnie's eyes against her will.

"About Saturday night…" Ronnie cooed.

"Yes?"

"Can we meet at the dance?"

There was a slight pause before Bud answered.

"The *dance?* Um…sure! Great! Uh, great! Yeah!"

"Okay, eight o'clock, see you there! *Bye-iee!*" Ronnie perked, and hung up the phone before Bud could know what hit him. There was something direct and powerful about Ronnie that I liked, but it also scared the *hell* out of me.

I wish we could communicate, I thought—then I thought—*I haven't really tried talking to her,* and suddenly wondered if I could, so I gave it a shot.

Ronnie?

"What?" she answered aloud.

You can hear me?

"Of course," she giggled. "I *am* you."

Oh, I didn't realize. Can we talk for a bit?

"Sure, I guess," she answered while she walked to the bathroom and searched my bottom drawer where I had dumped all the unused make-up Mom gave me over the years.

She rifled it, and sighed.

I need your help. Will you help me?

Ronnie went back to my closet and, rifling through my clothes next, let out an, "Ish!"

Ronnie, **please** *pay attention. Will you help me? Can we cooperate?*

M'kay," she replied, looking at herself in the mirror and tugging at my now ill-fitting bib overalls.

"But *you* have to do something for *me* first."

Since we shared a brain, I already knew exactly what she wanted.

Just then, the show ended and with the subtle crunching of bone and tissue, I returned to my old self. I looked in the mirror.

"Okay, Ronnie," I said aloud to my reflection. "I'll do it, but then you'll need to do your part too."

I went to my desk and, dialing in the combination, opened the metal box-safe I kept in the top drawer. All my college money I had been saving was in it and I had amassed a pretty impressive pile. I took a fairly serious wad of it out and stuffed it into my pocket.

I sighed, and returned to grab a second wad.

"You better come through for me, Ronnie," I warned.

I glanced at the clock. It was 4:23 PM. There was still about an hour before Dad got home. I snatched up the Walkman, attached the headphones, and headed for the door.

The drive to the shopping mall was a short one. Once there, I donned the headphones, turned on the recording of the game, slipped it in my top bib pocket and felt Ronnie crunch her way back to reality.

Here's the thing, Ronnie. You have the money I brought for you to spend and free rein until 5. When I say we're done, we head back to the car and the headphones come off. Deal?

"Deal," she replied with a grin.

Ronnie loved shopping every bit as much as I hated it, but her love of it was hard to resist, especially when I saw how cute she, and *I as her*, looked in the things she selected. And since I felt what she felt, it *felt* good. She hummed along with the various cheers and marching band's half-time moments running though our ears while she shopped, and even did a step or two along with it, to the amusement of other shoppers. Since I promised not to interfere, I took to studying her instead. She had the same innate aptitude for this that she had for cheerleading; she somehow automatically knew what colors of make-up and clothing to buy and wear to look her best. In its own weird, patently shallow way, it was impressive.

She settled on four full outfits: two skirts, two blouses, a pair of denim bell bottoms, and a pair of tan capri pants, but with several different colors of tights, tank tops, scarves, hair bands, and belts she managed to multiply the possibilities into a couple of dozen.

You're good at this, I complimented.

"Thanks! Now for a party dress."

She picked out a strapless powder-blue rayon slinky dress with matching heels. It fit her like a glove.

You look amazing.

"Thanks," she giggled, and posed in the mirror from different angles to see how it moved. She stopped with a jerk.

"Hey, I'm gonna buy *you* one," she whispered.

She went back to the rack of party dresses and picked out a corset-waist, strapless, pale peachy-orange one in my size with pleats and creamy-peach tulle underneath for volume. Although I had to admit its colors perfectly complimented my red hair and skin tone, it was something I'd never *ever* be caught dead in. I hated wasting hard-earned money on it, but I was already wasting money on all her other silly stuff, so I didn't argue.

And, well…it *was* kind of *sweet* of her to think of me.

I forced her to look at my watch and, seeing that it was ten to five, I suggested we head to the register and then to the car. Fortunately, Ronnie cooperated, and when the headphones came off and I was back to myself again, I zipped home.

At first break the next morning, I ducked into the girl's restroom at the far end of the mathematics wing—experience dictated it was the one that got the least use. Fortunately, the odds were on my side and I had it all to myself. I ducked into a stall and pulled out Ronnie's capri pants and fitted tank top with a wide belt and scarf that I'd seen her combine to her satisfaction while in the store fitting room, and quickly changed into it, stuffing my overalls into my daypack instead. I tried to button the waistband on the capri pants and couldn't, so I donned the headphones and click on the tape. In moments, my belly melted away and Ronnie easily zipped the front and buttoned the band. She clipped the Walkman to her belt and we were off.

All I need you to do is get him to sign this thing, I reminded her, while I forced control of her hands in order to extract the document from my daypack for her. Physically controlling Ronnie was a bit like having a puppy on a leash; it took a lot of effort and there was only so much control I could actually accomplish.

"You got it, hon," she whispered, as she took control again, dug around in my pack's front pocket, and glossed her lips.

We eventually found Mr. Randall outside his homeroom class, surrounded, as usual, by a gaggle of my female schoolmates. Ronnie approached and, skipping right up to him, dropped the document.

"Oopsie," she said, as she stooped to retrieve

it, giving Mr. Randall a nice view of her perfect little round capri-panted butt.

He stooped to help her.

They rose together, each holding a side of the document. His growing leer made me cringe, but I worked hard not to let it show so I wouldn't ruin Ronnie's routine, because so far, she seemed to know exactly what she was doing.

"Thanks," she giggled. "I'm such a little klutz."

"Anything I can do to help, I'm happy to," he baritoned back, letting go of the document.

"Oh, goodie—because I really need to get into your class this semester," Ronnie continued, with a head-tilt and the hint of a pout.

"Oh?"

"They said it was already full, but I guess if you sign this, I can still get in," she cooed, lifting the document up to just below her cleavage so as not to obscure his view.

Good girl.

Mr. Randall smiled. Without taking his eyes off Ronnie, he grabbed a pen from his shirt pocket, took the document, slapped it up against the wall, glanced sideways at it and signed, then handed it back to her.

"Looking forward to having you in my class," he said with a pearly grin, clicking his pen several times before putting it back in his pocket.

I see! You wouldn't do it for me but you'll do it for her! I groused, but then realized too late that, in my angry internal outburst, I'd just inadvertently forced my words of incredulity out of Ronnie's mouth!

"Wha...?"

"Gotta run...thanks, Mr. Randall!" I perked, in the best impersonation of Ronnie I could muster, as I made her bounce off down the hall and away before I screwed things up any more.

While I tucked the signed document back in my daypack and breathed a sigh of relief, Ronnie wrested control back again to skip over to join a group of the most popular girls in the school. They welcomed her immediately and Felicia complimented her on her cute outfit, she complimented each of them on the same, and between their continuing chatter about hair, make-up, and boys, coupled with listening to a football game in my head, I kinda had to tune it all out.

I was used to being an invisible observer so it didn't really bother me. I also figured I owed Ronnie this moment and, to be truthful, it was a bit of the fulfillment of every plain-Jane's fantasy to be in with the in crowd and have them all liking on me. Even though it wasn't really me they were liking on, and the stuff they were talking about was pretty lame—to be honest—I *emotionally* felt everything Ronnie felt, and it felt *nice* to be liked. I remembered reading somewhere that when women socialize with other women, studies suggested that more of the hormone oxytocin is released, which counters stress and produces a calming effect, and that may have been part of what I was feeling. Whatever the physiological process, it made me realize how much of a parched social desert my life generally was, and how much I really did long for friendship and the acceptance of my schoolmates.

It took a lot of effort, but I finally forced Ronnie to glance at my watch. Break was ending soon, so I reminded her that we needed to go change back. She completely ignored me until I also reminded her that if we didn't go change, *she'd* have to sit though AP calculus instead of me—that did the trick.

The next few days were weirder for me than Ronnie, in the sense that, other than on game days and rally schedules, Ronnie ceased to exist unless I deliberately released her. But I found I was opting to release her more often. There were things she could do that I simply could not, like getting into Mr. Randall's class, for example, and although it meant losing control of myself while being Ronnie, I found the power of being pretty intoxicating—and addictive.

A perfect example was when I'd forgotten my lunch and was in a hurry to get through a very long lunch line fast so I could review for my Calculus quiz. I noticed Tanya and Linda Burke almost at the front, so I ducked away, returned as Ronnie, and was welcomed to cut in. Of course, once Ronnie was in charge, studying was out and chatting with the girls ate up the entire lunch hour.

And, I am embarrassed to admit that later that afternoon I even unleashed Ronnie right before water polo practice just so that I could sit in the poolside bleachers and be surrounded by the swimsuit-clad team while they all flirted with her and chatted her up. It was the hormonal high it yielded that made me do it, I guess, and the feeling of being physically desired. I noticed Lainey and Dinah watching me as they passed by outside the chain link fence surrounding the pool area. I hadn't seen nor heard from Lainey since our talk and was curious what she was thinking, but not curious enough to initiate contact again...yet.

Then Bud came by and when he saw Ronnie, he came to sit with her for a while. I was severely conflicted about what I felt, which was an incredible sexual rush from his physical desire for her, but it was coupled with my own internal feelings of betrayal: my betrayal of him for teasing attention out of him with Ronnie, and his of me, for lusting after her instead of me.

As I expected, Mr. Randall never really caught on to the fact that I was the one attending his class and not Ronnie because, *natch*, I was invisible to him.

It was a dangerous game I was playing, because I could only barely control Ronnie once she was in charge. It usually took a strong force of emotions or anger to motivate her body back in my own control, and she was such an energetic force to begin with, I wasn't always successful. And arguing with her generally did no good at all, because she hadn't a brain in her head.

Another downside, or maybe an upside, depending on how I looked at it at any given moment, was that when she left and I was back to my old self after a round of her physical cheering and gymnastics, *my* body was the one having to live through the recovery. I was not generally a very physically active person and we were sharing the same body. One night after practice I ached so badly that I had to soak in a bathtub with Epsom salts for a half an hour to ease the pain. The upside was that her workouts and daintier eating habits were forcing me to lose weight and tone up, because when I caught a glimpse of myself in the mirror after my bath, I was really surprised how much better my body was already looking. I had to admit it—it made me smile.

The major problem with my drug-of-choice being transforming into Ronnie was that my schoolwork began seriously suffering. I actually got my first B on the paper I rushed out at the last second for AP English and I had gotten two wrong answers on my first Calculus quiz she kept me from reviewing for. It was still an A, but Mr. Waxman's puzzled look as he handed me my paper back felt like an omen.

Chapter Fourteen

HOME WORK

Saturday arrived with a flurry of activity brought on by one of Mom's book-promotion events. As Richie, Robbie, and I stood in the foyer with Dad, who was laden with two large boxes of her books and fliers, she handed each of us our list of chores for the day followed by a kiss.

Mom was the only one in the room who looked happy.

"Your dad and I will be home by six," she informed us, "so you'll have plenty of time to finish your chores."

My brothers scanned their lists and immediately began negotiating with each other.

"Ugh...I got bathrooms," Richie groused, glancing at Robbie's list. "I'll trade you bathrooms for vacuuming."

"Uhn-uh. I like vacuuming. For dishes."

"For dishes? How about bathrooms and mopping the hallway floor for dishes?"

"For dishes *and* dusting!"

Mom was about to interject but shook her head at their antics, opting instead to defer the responsibility to me.

"Rhonda, you're in charge. Just make sure they get it all done and don't goof off."

Dad, who was being patient despite the heavy boxes, interjected, "Rose honey, let's go."

I opened the door for him and he waddled toward the car. Mom followed, scanning her Filofax, and turned back.

"Oh, Rhonda," she added. "Don't forget our quality time tonight."

Shoot.

I'd totally forgotten about the goofy "quality time" thing she had invented for a chapter of her book and now felt obligated to do with me—and this was game night with the dance to follow. Whether I liked it or not, I'd be Ronnie all evening. There was no way out.

I had to do the unthinkable.

"I can't do it tonight, Mom. I'm busy. Sorry."

Dad dropped the boxes next to the car with a thud and turned back. My brothers' heads poked out the door.

Everyone's eyes were on Mom.

"Busy?" The word leaked out of her.

The birds seemed to stop chirping in the trees. A cone of silence descended upon our house. Mom stood motionless for a second or two, her head tilted to one side, her eyebrows raised. Then came the pursed lips and a head shake, like one you would do when the thing you just heard can't possibly be what you just heard.

"No." she said, then she turned and added, as she headed for the car, "It's only an hour. I'm sure you can make time for that."

"No. I...I really *can't.*"

We all watched Mom's back straighten and at this point Robbie retreated back in the house to watch from the safety of the living room window. Richie looked at me with a kind of nervous admiration and, although he took a few steps back too, stayed, probably hoping for fireworks.

Mom returned to face me square on, now wearing a tight smile.

"I make time in my schedule, which is very busy

right now, I might add, and you can't be bothered?" She held up her day planner and pointed. "We've had our quality time scheduled for weeks. *I've* made it a priority, and I guess I'm, well...a little surprised...and *hurt*...that this apparently isn't a priority for *you*."

"Something came up...unexpectedly. Look, I'm sorry, but I really *can't* get out of it, Mom. Besides...it's important to me."

"More important than your *mother?* Than *us?*"

"Mom," I huffed in exasperation. *"Please..."*

"Okay," she clipped, putting her day planner into her purse with a crisp snap, "so, what is this *all-important* thing that means *more to you* than nourishing our mother/daughter relationship?"

What the heck—I figured I was already in over my head so deep I didn't even try to fake my way through this.

"If you must know, I need to attend the Talbot football game tonight."

Out of the corner of my eye I saw Dad sit down on the boxes and put his head in his hands. It was now Richie's turn to duck back into the house.

"Oh...a football game." Mom paused for effect, then added, "I never realized you were such a devoted fan."

I'm not really sure what happened next or why. I think it was partly due to her attempt at emotional manipulation followed by her sarcastic tone on top of my own frustration and lack of control over Ronnie that made me do it. But I lost it.

I lost it *big-time*.

"How would *you* have any idea what *I* like or don't like?!" I growled back, launching each of my words at her like ballistic missiles. "Unless you read it in your damned day-planner it doesn't exist!? I have a life too, you know! And when we do talk, it's all about *you* and what *you're doing* anyway! You *never* pay *any* attention to what I'm doing unless it's something you can use for a chapter in your *stupid* book! *My life is not a book!* It's real! And, *sorry*, but sometimes things don't fit into nice, neat little tidy chapters...or, or categories, they just...happen! **Things just happen!** And...oh, you don't care! **You just don't care!**"

I turned on my heels, went back into the house, and slammed the front door.

I stood in the foyer with my back to it, immobile.

My brothers stood in the living room, staring at me, also frozen. We eventually heard the car doors close and the sound of the car leaving.

"What brought *that* on?" Robbie whispered to Richie.

"Hormones," Richie whispered back.

"Do your chores and *stay outta my hair!*" I snarled, as I took my own list and started cleaning.

To their credit, the guys knew not to mess with me, so chores went without a hitch. The only incident of note was when I heard a loud, "Aaak!" followed by a clamor of falling debris. I ran to find Robbie in a heap on the stair landing. He had tried to carry too much up the stairs all at once and his collection of toys, my daypack, and a full basket of clean laundry were now a hodge-podge mess strewn about the stairs, landing, and foyer.

He also had a nasty bump rising on his forehead and looked on the verge of tears, but was otherwise okay, so I didn't scold him. Instead, I grabbed the basket and started refolding clothes while he replaced the contents of my daypack and reorganized his toys. I approached with the basket just as he replaced the voice tape into the back of his Teddy Ruxpin and hugged it close.

"C'mon," I said, giving him a hug, "Let's put this stuff away and get some ice for your head."

By mid-afternoon we were all done with our chores. The boys went out in the backyard, doubtless to either bury something dead, set something on fire, or build something dangerous. I retreated to my room. I was operating on fumes at this point but decided to clean and organize my own room too, hoping an orderly environment might buoy my sullen mood. Once everything was neat as a pin, I took all the cleaning supplies and rags to the utility room and returned to my room to finally relax.

One look in the mirror and my day's general depression worsened. My hair had become a jumbled bundle of clumps, my natural frown seemed more pronounced than usual, and I was badly in need of a shower, so I stripped off and took a nice, long hot one, conditioning my hair and carefully combing every last kink out of it. I even used some of the face moisturizer Ronnie had bought, then I went back to my bedroom to put on fresh clothes.

Ronnie's party dress, the one she would wear to the dance, hung there. I took it out and held it up against my bathrobe. Its sleekness and powder-blue color didn't suit me. I replaced it and took out the dress Ronnie had picked out for me, the peachy-orange colored one, holding that up instead. I closed my eyes and pictured myself in it, dancing with Bud. The mixture of emotions this brought up wasn't helping, so I tucked it back into the closet and took out slacks and a tee, tossed them on the bed, and closed the closet.

I dropped my robe and crossed to my underwear drawer to get some panties. When I turned around, I caught a glimpse of my own naked body in the mirrored closet doors and for just a nanosecond, my own reflection startled me, because I didn't immediately recognize the girl I saw there. Being Ronnie had forced me to eat and exercise differently, and with my damp hair still in soft loops rather than its usual kinky mounds, for just that one split-second, I wondered who the hell that pretty naked girl across the room, who looked a lot like a younger version of my beautiful mom, was.

Did I say pretty?

It was...kinda *true* though, until I realized it was just me after all.

Being Ronnie was doing odd things to me. I mean, aside from the big, freaky transformational events. She had made me much more aware of my normal body, for sure. And I noticed she was teaching it to move more gracefully, mostly through her training muscle memory into me rather than anything conscious on my part; it wasn't something I had even thought about, but I realized right then that my posture had improved since she came along and that lately my figure appeared to have more of a bust and less of a waist because I wasn't slouching as much. But even after mistakenly seeing myself as pretty just then, I still knew I *wasn't* pretty, so I shook it off.

I threw on my panties, slacks, bra, and a tee and crossed to my bookshelf to grab last year's yearbook.

I took it to the bed and sat.

Propped up against the headboard on my pillows, I flipped to the section devoted to the sports teams, specifically to the half-page picture of Bud next to last year's first-string quarterback, Frank Martell. Frank was beefy and handsome in his own way, but lacked the classic, chiseled beauty of Bud's more ideal proportions. There was a signature next to Bud's picture: "Always your bud, Bud."

I sighed, flopping down with the open book across my chest, as my mind reeled in contradictions.

I like being Ronnie, but I'm not Ronnie. Ronnie is prettier than I am and so... life is just...easier for her, but GOD...she has no brains! I'm becoming addicted to being her though, I can feel it. I know I need to get rid of her, somehow, but still don't know how. A part of me wants to be her rather than me—but...how stupid is that?!

And I like Bud, but he likes Ronnie, not me, so to have Bud, I need to be Ronnie? But if Ronnie gets Bud, I still don't really get Bud...Ronnie does. And I don't have a way to stay Ronnie even if I wanted to, so she can't really have Bud either.

And if I had to choose whether to always be me or Ronnie, of course—I want to be me. But right now, I can't choose to be only me either and have to be both of us. And tonight, I'm gonna have to be Ronnie whether I like it or not...

Ugh.

It was just after sunset and I must have dozed off while fretting, because I didn't hear my bedroom door creak open.

I didn't hear Richie and Robbie sneak in and approach my bed. I didn't even feel Richie carefully lift the yearbook from my chest, or see him point at the picture of Bud, or hear both of them giggle and make kissy-noises.

I only awoke when Robbie had my upper and lower lips between his fingers, making me mouth to his impersonation of me saying, "Oh, Bud...I love you! You're so wonderful! I'll love you forever!" followed by more kissy noises and their giggles.

"Knock it off, you little creeps!" I snarled, bolting upright. They both fell on the floor in fits of laughter. I flopped back down on my bed and pounded madly with all four limbs in frustration, and to keep myself from pounding on them.

Just then, a soft shaft of light slipped through the window, followed by a muffled and distant, echoing thunk: the stadium lights at Talbot High came on, in preparation for the game.

And, right on cue, my body lurched and went rigid, followed by the transformational crunching of cartilage and bone.

I glimpsed over to see my brothers slowly rise to their feet, back away, and stare agape, as they watched my belly cinch and fingernails lengthen, my hair soften, and my breasts fill my tee.

They stood frozen in horror until they saw Ronnie sit up, toss her blond hair from her eyes, and giggle, "Hey, li'l guys. What's up?"

That's when they bolted from the room.

Ronnie bounced off the bed, clicked on the light, took one look at what I was wearing, and let out an, "Ish."

She immediately changed into one of her own outfits: the denim bell bottoms and white peplum blouse. Then she dumped all my books and papers out of my daypack into a heap on the bed and carefully folded her blue dress for the dance, packing it and her matching shoes neatly inside.

Keep the Walkman in there, you might need it at the dance, I reminded, and she extracted it and the loose cassette tape from the pile on the bed to stuff into the front pocket.

Meanwhile, I heard a car outside pull up and my parents enter the house to be confronted by my crazed brothers racing out the front door. A muffled exchange followed.

"Hold on! Where do you two think you're going?!" Dad scolded.

"Run for your lives!" Richie shouted.

"Rhonda's a pod-person! Rhonda's a pod-person!" Robbie repeated, his voice now coming from the front yard.

Richie's voice joined him in the front yard, screaming, "We're not kidding this time, Dad! Go upstairs and look!"

I heard Dad say to Mom, "I'll take care of them. You go have your talk."

Then I heard the front door close and Dad's voice outside, coaxing my brothers to come to him or there'd be hell to pay. This was followed by Mom's footfalls on the stairs.

Shoot.

Without thinking I was somehow able to wrest control of Ronnie and turn out the lights. I dove onto the bed and scrambled under my bedspread mere seconds before hearing the door to my room click open a crack.

Don't you dare say a word, I warned Ronnie as I wrestled to keep control, even clasping a hand over her mouth. *Let me do the talking.*

"Honey...? Can I come in...?"

Ronnie pulled the one hand loose with the other and perked, "Sure."

I fought back, pulling the bedspread up over her head and tighter around her. Through a fold in the spread I could see Mom step into the room. She briefly glanced my way, sighed, and then turned away, looking out the window instead of at me as she spoke.

"I realize you're probably still mad at me and in no mood to talk but I've been worried all day about how upset and angry you were this morning."

Her voice was soft and sounded sincere. I wanted very much to believe her, but she was right: I was still angry.

"I thought about it a lot and you know, you were *right*, sweetheart," she continued, "I haven't paid much attention to you lately. But, well...it seems like you always have everything under control...."

Ronnie chose that ironic moment to take complete control back from me, sit up, and pull her head free from under the bedspread in order to look across at herself in the closet mirror and fuss with her tousled hair. I tried in vain to wrest control back, but it was no use. While Ronnie ignored me *and* Mom, I continued to listen.

"...you've always been so sure of yourself. You know what you want and how to get it, so I've felt it best just to leave you alone and not butt in."

Mom moved closer to the window, momentarily distracted by the mayhem taking place down on our front lawn, where I could hear Dad shout, "No more, boys! Not another word!"

"And when the idea for my book came along, it was a real opportunity to make a name for myself and really progress my career. Which helps us all. The whole family. That's why...I expected everyone's full support—which is why I was, well...a little surprised and hurt...."

Here it is, I thought. I could hear the subtle shift in her tone as Mom played the tried and true guilt card. She even paused for effect—waiting for my reaction.

Ronnie, on the other hand, wasn't paying any attention to her; she was French braiding her hair.

I convinced myself that my guilt switch was still securely in the off position and continued to listen.

A clamor arose from the entry downstairs. The front door slammed. Several pairs of footfalls stomped up the stairs and in the direction of Richie and Robbie's room, followed by another door slam.

Getting no reaction, Mom tried a second volley. "...I mean, the extra money I'm making with this book will come in real handy when you enter college next year."

Money-guilt too, Mom?

Ronnie still didn't react, nor could I.

Reading a non-response as the silent treatment, Mom eventually sighed, looked at the floor and conceded me the moment, adding, "Anyway, I want you to know I understand the changes you are going through right now...I *really do*, honey."

Ha.

My internal scoffing laugh came out of Ronnie's mouth as a soft giggling, "Ha," causing Mom's posture to droop even more. She crossed to the door, still without looking at Ronnie, and added, "So, will you forgive me and we can start fresh? I really *am* sorry."

Ronnie shrugged her shoulders and perked back, "Sounds neat to me."

Neat?

"Neat?" Mom answered along with me. "Well... *good* then," she finished as she left the room, closing the door behind her.

It was my turn to sigh with relief. I suggested to Ronnie we lock the door and thankfully she agreed to do so. As she did, I could hear my parents conversing in whispers in the hallway outside my door—Dad must have been eavesdropping.

"She seemed in a good mood. Your talk must have gone well."

"Um-hum, fine...*I think*. Where are the boys?"

"In their room, grounded, until they give up this latest nonsense. They claim Rhonda isn't Rhonda, but that she's been replaced by an alien replicant."

Chapter Fifteen

MIXED TAPE

Having never attended a football game before, I was definitely along for the ride and only passively observing while Ronnie did her thing. She and the other cheerleaders roused the crowd while Bud, Durk, and the rest of the team tossed the football around, grunted, smashed, kicked, got sweaty and grass-stained, and ran their way to an impressive 15-0 lead in no time flat.

"Go, Tigers! Bury the Groundhogs! Bury the Groundhogs...!"

Ronnie and the girls repeated their "Bury the Groundhogs" chant while the crowd in the stands joined them. There was a primitive glee that made me glad no real tigers were in our arena and that they were only using a pod-shaped pigskin ball rather than an opposing team member's severed head.

I directly experienced Ronnie's enthusiasm and adrenalin rush and soon I found myself getting emotionally caught up in the game. I *loved* seeing Bud in action—his athletic abilities were impressive and I soon found I wanted him to triumph. I hated admitting this to myself though, because I had always felt that team sports were beneath my intellect, and Bud's too, for that matter, which then made me feel embarrassed and a little guilty for not realizing until now what a snob I was being and how unfair it was to him.

Of course, the dose of humble-pie didn't stop my mind from thinking that this whole, "Bury the Groundhogs!" chant was pretty damned idiotic, given the fact that actual groundhogs live underground, so to bury them would likely not punish them in the least—but such is the downside of having an active mind full of mostly useless information with a tendency to question everything.

Our team made another touchdown and Bud added a two-point conversion right before halftime. Then both teams headed to their respective locker rooms with their coaches and the next thing I knew I was in the middle of the field being tossed around and helping toss around other girls as the marching band ran circles around us playing, "Band on the Run." While stuck in the middle of a pyramid of girls I glanced at the stands, observing that almost everyone out there seemed far more interested in surrounding the concession stand like starved ants on a fresh picnic spread than watching our halftime show.

The thought of food made my stomach growl and I realized I'd not had any dinner, having urged Ronnie to slip out my bedroom window to drop from the roof eave in order to avoid being seen by my parents or the sibs on my way to the game.

We eventually cleared the field and the second half opened with Durk fumbling the ball on the very first play and one of the Groundhogs turning his fumble into a touchdown. Their kicker added a point and things got more intense after that. Durk went after the guy who had retrieved the fumble and knocked the wind out of him—the guy took it in stride, but the whole game felt darker than my more favorable impression of the first half had been.

Einstein never explained it, but time is variable in the experiencing of it, because, although the second half was just as long as the first, it seemed to fly by to me. As the clock ran down and we had possession, Bud was able to break through their line to almost miraculously eke out one more touchdown from our own thirty-yard line, sending Ronnie and the cheerleaders into leaping fits and the stands into a standing, foot-stomping eruption of cheers for him.

Bud, hoisted on the shoulders of his teammates, was paraded around the field, followed by the marching band, playing the Bee Gee's, "You Should Be Dancing."

As Bud passed by, he shot an ear-to-ear grin right at me—or more accurately, at Ronnie—and tossed her the game ball.

She caught it, kissed it, and winked back.

Ronnie, showered and toweled off, did her makeup, and slipped effortlessly into her party dress. We looked in the mirror to final-check things.

She smiled with pleasure and with good reason. She was a knock-out.

How can I possibly compete with her for Bud's attention?

If the town of Stepford had created a perfect teenager, she'd be it.

We were entering the unknown though, for I had no idea if the spell would consider this after-game dance a required event for Ronnie to exist in, or if it would transform her back and leave *me* in a real pickle.

Bud stood just outside the gym door, waiting for us.

He held out a box with a corsage in it, and Ronnie giggled with glee.

"Thanks, Bud," she perked, opening the plastic lid and carefully extracting the butter-yellow orchid inside.

Bud helped her pin it on.

This is pretty corny, I thought, and then followed that thought with, *Bud thinks it is too, I'll bet.*

I glanced at him for any signs of it, but he wasn't letting on. Instead, he continued the corn by extending his arm and asking, "Shall we?"

And the corn didn't end there. Nope. It was only the beginning.

"The Love Boat," painted on a banner across the gym entrance to match the TV show's title design, announced the dance's theme. An up-ramp outside the gym entrance had been engineered by the dance committee so we could then walk down a gangplank once inside. Bud had to duck his head to get through the shortened doorway, due to the ramps. He laced fingers with Ronnie to give her high-heeled feet more stability going down, and I swooned at his touch, almost making her stumble.

Apparently, the dance committee had even talked Mr. Wexler, the geometry teacher, into dressing up as Captain Stubing, likely because he was as bald as Gavin MacLeod. Ms. Lyle, dressed as Julie, stood by his side, greeting each couple.

"Ahoy, step aboard the Love Boat," he emoted, playing the role as if he had been asked to double for the real show, which made me think life as a geometry teacher must be pretty boring for him to be so into it.

"Thanks, Mr. Wexler," Bud replied.

"It's Captain Stubing tonight," he corrected, with a chuckle and a wink.

"Aye-aye, Captain," Bud returned, with a salute.

Ronnie giggled.

"Refreshments are on the sundeck, enjoy your cruise," Ms. Lyle added with a little less ham-acting than Mr. Wexler, gesturing to the far end of the room where a platform with snacks and a drink table had been erected in front of a huge butcher paper mural of a sunset over the ocean pinned to the wall behind it.

"Cool, thanks," Bud replied.

"Let's dance," Ronnie suggested, tugging Bud onto the dance floor.

While the DJ played "Love Will Keep Us Together," Bud and Ronnie jerked rhythmically around the floor. I tried to feel Ronnie's rhythms as they did, so I could learn some dance moves from her. Everybody looked pretty goofy doing it though, which made me feel like I had nothing to worry about if I ever had to fake it.

Bud's dancing was only goofy enough to make him look even more adorable.

We danced past the sundeck where Tanya and Linda stood near the punchbowl with their dates. They smiled and waved to Ronnie, who waved back. The song finished with us stopping right next to Mr. Randall and Ms. Tarbo, who were on chaperone duty.

Mr. Randall leered at Ronnie and gave us a, "Hi, kids."

"Evening, Mr. Randall, Ms. Tarbo," Bud responded, politely.

The music launched into, "Baby, I'm A Want You," and Mr. Randall, glancing my way, asked," Do you think it would be considered inappropriate for a chaperone to ask for a dance?"

Ms. Tarbo, who had been looking the other way, mistakenly thought he was talking to her. She turned with a grin, took his hand, and dragged him to the dance floor with the reply, "Not at all, Bob...I thought you'd *never* ask."

My own internal chuckle managed to make Ronnie laugh.

Bud took my hand, slipped his other hand around my waist, and led me to the floor. I say *me* because I was so emotionally caught up in the moment I could no longer tell if it was me or Ronnie dancing with him. Bud's warm cheek nuzzled my ear, and he whispered, "Having a good time?"

"Yes," I answered, hearing my words come out as Ronnie's voice, "I've always dreamed of going to a dance."

"You've never been to a dance before? I'd think a girl like you would have been asked a bunch of times."

"I was asked before," I continued, "but I didn't want to go."

"Why not?"

"Wrong boy," I explained. "I wanted to go with you."

"I'm glad you did."

It was strange. I had *no* idea why I felt so *completely* in control of Ronnie at this particular moment, but as Bud and I leaned in for a kiss Ronnie suddenly woke up from her stupor, broke free and spun in glee, interrupting it.

"Isn't high school *great*, Bud?" she perked. "I hope it goes on forever!"

Bud laughed, if a bit uncomfortably. He took her hands in his again, radiating a look of confusion as he walked her off the floor.

"You are the only girl I've ever met who could say something like that and sound sincere. But we can't stay at Talbot forever."

It was now Ronnie's turn to look confused.

"What do you plan to do after you graduate?" Bud asked.

"I haven't thought about it," Ronnie answered, truthfully.

Bud looked a bit frustrated, but pressed on.

"Well, what do you want to do in life?"

"Be a cheerleader of course, *silly*," she sighed and rolled her eyes, as if stating the obvious—and for her, she was.

Bud's look melted into disappointment.

"I'll get us some punch," he offered, and headed to the sundeck. Ronnie sat on one of the open bleachers nearby, smooothed her dress and stared up at the disco ball spinning in the center of the room, humming along to the music and smiling blissfully—nothing much in the way of thinking going on that I could discern—meanwhile my own mind reeled.

*Okay, I know **he** knows she's vapid, but why doesn't that matter? Why **her** and not **me**?*

I heard a muffled conversation behind me, underneath the bleachers, so, curious, I forced Ronnie to turn and peer back between the riser seats. She didn't resist.

It was the Geekster Club trio, huddled in the shadows at the back of the risers, near one of the wall sockets where the DJ's equipment was plugged in.

Ted pointed to a second socket full of plugs further down the wall.

"A building of this size *always* has a high capacity voltage regulator. They obviously don't realize either socket could easily handle all the wattage output."

"Except that this gym was built in the 1930's by the W.P.A., when the standard output requirements were significantly lower," Fred countered, "and unless the building was upgraded in the interim, then obviously the use of separate plugs is necessitated."

"Care to wager?"

"You're on."

"Here we are," Bud said, as he returned with two

plastic glasses full of punch.

He and Ronnie tap-clinked plastic.

"To the best date ever," Bud whispered as his eyes filled with hopeful affection.

My heart sank as the imaginary me burst into tears. Bud was so *gone* on Ronnie. His eyes said it all and I suddenly felt very depressed.

"Ronnie? You alright? You're...*crying*," Bud said.

"I am?" Ronnie replied, touching what must have been *my* tears rolling down her cheek.

"Is something wrong?"

Ronnie took a tissue from her pocket and carefully daubed the tear away. She smiled sweetly, leaned in, and cooed, "Nope. Nothing at all."

Bud leaned in too. I could feel his warmth, then, the warmth of his breath as our lips approached, about to embrace...

A loud pop was followed by a shower of sparks spraying from under the bleachers, making us jump up, interrupting our kiss. We reeled back further as the room went dark and the smell of electric smoke hit our noses.

From out of the darkness under the bleachers we heard Fred yell, "*Told* ya!"

The DJ started cursing, the teachers tried to hush him and calm the room, and someone else yelled, "Get a flashlight!"

Bud grabbed my hand.

"Let's get out of here."

Bud pulled into The Malt Shop parking lot, where, in an earlier age, roller skate-wearing carhops would have served customers. He parked, hopped out, rounded his car and leaned in through my open window.

"So...what can I get you, miss?"

"Cheeseburger, fries and a shake," Ronnie perked back, sounding exactly like a TV commercial.

"You got it. Back in a flash," Bud replied, dashing for the door.

And just as I started to wonder how long Ronnie would remain Ronnie, I felt the change-back begin.

"Oh, fer the love of...*Shoot!*"

My breasts shrank as the waist of Ronnie's dress stretched more tautly to accommodate my own. I twisted the rear-view mirror in order to confirm the rapid returning of my own face and curly red hair.

Oh, god. What do I do now? Should I make a run for it?

Then I remembered my back-up plan.

The tape!

I leaned over into the back seat and scrambled for Ronnie's purse, extracting the Walkman and tape recording of the football halftime. I donned the headphones, popped the tape into the Walkman, and clicked it on.

"Hello. I'm Teddy Ruxpin and I'd like to tell you a story..."

What the...?

My mind flashed back to try to make sense of it.

Omigod—Robbie must have mixed up our tapes when he dropped everything on the stairs when we were cleaning....

There was a rap on the car door and I jerked up to see Linda Burke staring in the window at me. She looked me up and down and made a face.

"Um, what are *you* doing in Bud's car?" she asked with a huff of incredulity. Tanya Sweet and her date approached to peer in at me too, followed by other curious couples.

I yanked the headphones off and tried to smile as casually as I could at her. I looked around the car's interior, then back at Linda.

"Well, *gee*...it looks like I'm sitting here, doesn't it? Yup, I'm sitting here."

"Where's Bud?" she puzzled, looking around.

The crowd of after-dancers kept steadily thickening.

"Inside getting us some burgers, if it's any business of yours. Which it's *not*."

I rolled up my window just as someone mumbled, "Bud's dating *Rhonda Glock?*" and a couple of people laughed.

I was about to lock the doors when I decided a better option was to make a run for it *before* Bud got back and found me there instead of Ronnie, and then try to make up some excuse to him later, so I pushed my door open and scrambled out, stumbling in Ronnie's silly heels, ending up on my knees, and evoking a roar of laughter.

And then, as if right on cue in the momentary disaster movie that was my life, Bud returned carrying the burger bag and drink holder.

I looked up at him and he looked down at me.

The crowd went silent and stepped back to give us room as they watched, rapt.

I rose to my feet and, not knowing *what* to say to Bud, threw out the first thing that came into my head.

"I'm just gonna run...to the ladies' room."

Someone in the crowd tossed something.

A condom packet landed at Bud's feet.

"Have fun tonight guys," the college guy that Linda was dating said with a smirk as the snickering crowd began to disburse.

Bud and I stood frozen. He stared at me with a blank look that was hard to read. He didn't look mad or hurt or confused or even amused. It was inscrutable. Blank.

Passionless.

When I finally broke free of his gaze, I noticed we were now alone.

I then wondered how the look on my face appeared to him, as I wasn't yet sure what *I* felt either.

Mostly embarrassed, and maybe...guilty?

Bud walked over to the hood of the car and set the burgers and drinks on it. He rested his hands on the hood and leaned in, took a deep breath, and turned to face me again. This time, I could easily read the anger there.

"Ron, *what*...is going on?!"

I opened my mouth to reply but nothing came out before Bud continued.

"I mean...is this some kind of a sick joke? Because if it is, it's not funny."

I still didn't know what to say so I just shook my head.

Bud glanced around and then back at me.

"Where the hell's Ronnie? Was she in on this?"

"You...*might* say that," I mumbled with a shrug as I stared at the ground.

I heard Bud sigh, followed by silence. I glanced up. This time he looked hurt. And still angry.

"Do I get *any* kind of explanation?"

I lifted Ronnie's dress so I wouldn't trip on it and approached Bud. I figured now was as good a time as any to try to let him in on the truth.

But how do I even begin?

"First of all," I offered, "please believe me, none

of this was meant to hurt you. You're the last person in the world I...*we*...I would want to hurt. It's just...there's this thing going on with Ronnie...and me...and, well... it all went *wrong*. It's very hard to explain, but *trust me*..."

"Trust you!? I oughta *strangle you!*" he snarled, making me reel back. "I don't get you, Ron. Rhonda Glock: straight-A student, slash, practical joker? What am I *supposed* to think, huh? You're standing here in Ronnie's dress, I'm standing here with cold burgers and warm shakes, Ronnie's gone *God knows where*, and the rest of the city is laughing their *heads* off at us. Me *trust you?* I've just been *humiliated!*"

"Hey, well...I'm embarrassed too, ya know! If you'd just let me *explain* you'll understand how *I* feel..."

"How *you* feel? Oh. Right."

Bud let out a grunt, folded his arms across his chest, and shook his head at me.

"What the hell happened to you, Ron? You're the one who is supposed to be smart and stable. You're the one friend I always depend on. Then you *embarrass* me like this!"

Now it was my turn to cross my arms and snort back.

"Oh. *Embarrass* you? You mean in front of your 'friends' like Linda or Durk and the rest of that vapid crowd? Aren't you forgetting that when you're with them, *I* don't even *exist?!* That I'm *invisible?* I'm just here to help you with your school work and then vanish, *huh*—isn't *that* my role, Bud? We can be friends as long as none of *them* ever knows it? As long as no one *sees* you with me? Because God knows, to be *seen* with *me* is such an *embarrassment!*"

"Wait," Bud stammered, "I..."

"I'm sorry, it won't **ever** happen again," I sobbed as I hoisted Ronnie's dress and hobbled off in her stupid shoes leaving Bud to grunt and pound his car hood in frustration.

The long walk back to the school parking lot and my car, once I removed Ronnie's toe-crushing high-heels and walked barefooted, gave me time to cool off.

My mind felt as numb as my cold, bare feet.

I climbed into the dark car and changed into Ronnie's street clothes, stuffed Ronnie's dance dress into my daypack, drove home, and parked in the driveway.

The football, the one Bud tossed to Ronnie after the game, lay cradled in the passenger seat next to me.

I picked it up, held it to my chest, and had a good, long, deep cry.

When all my tears were spent, I pulled some tissues from the box Mom kept in the passenger foot well and mopped my face and nose. Some of Ronnie's make up came off in the tissue, so I wiped harder. I wanted to be rid of every trace of her. I turned the mirror to look, only to confirm that I'd managed to smear her damned mascara into two blackened eyes—I looked like a monster movie zombie, which first made me chuckle, then cry again.

When I finally did climb out of the car, I noticed a light still on in my brothers' upstairs bedroom window. Their two silhouettes were framed there, eerily watching me, so I waved and held up the game ball to show it off to them.

This caused them to jerk back and snap the curtains shut.

Great, that's one good thing to come out of this mess, the brats will leave me alone.

I entered the house quietly so as not to awaken our parents—I was in no mood to talk to anyone. As I climbed the stairs, however, I heard my brothers' door creak open. When I reached the upstairs landing and looked down the hall, Richie and Robbie stood, side by side, now silhouetted in their doorway. Richie held a baseball bat and Robbie, wearing a football helmet, was armed with Richie's tennis racquet.

I guess I must have looked a bit frightening with my blackened and red-from-crying eyes. I shook my head and laughed, too tired and emotionally drained to try to explain or to make sense of myself, my transformation, or any of it to them. It actually felt good to laugh.

I held up the ball.

Richie gasped and whispered, "A *pod*."

"It's not a pod, it's the *game ball*, Richie. You guys want it?" I offered.

They both took a step back.

"Whatever you do, *don't fall asleep*," Richie whispered to Robbie before they ducked back into their room and locked their door.

Chapter Sixteen

BODY SNATCHER

I knew it was stupid—that it wasn't a logical, sensible, or well-reasoned response to my situation—but I woke up feeling energized to fight back: against Bud, against Ronnie, against Mom, and all of Talbot High too. But mostly, I suppose, against my own view of myself.

Just because everyone and everything is telling me I'm not pretty enough, I don't have to accept it, at least not without a fight.

So, I made the conscious decision then and there to reject everyone else's conclusion.

I decided that I *was* pretty, and that no one else saw me that way because I never really made the effort to see myself nor present myself as such. So, I took my shower, conditioned and brushed out my hair, and rather than my usual overalls and tee, I dressed in pegged chino trousers, a crisp white blouse, and my ruddy-red canvas flats that Mom bought for me last summer because she thought they almost perfectly matched the color of my hair.

I scanned Ronnie's make up, but rejected the idea, aspiring to be a "natural beauty" rather than a phony-baloney painted one, although after seeing my undeniably flat, pale face staring back at me, I relented to wearing a whisper of her rouge powder with just a thin hint of soft peach-colored lipstick.

Okay, that's not bad.

I turned this way and that with a hand mirror to see myself from various angles. The clothes and face now looked good, but my hair just kind of sat there. It was curling in soft ringlets, rather than frizzing, but it had too much volume and no real shape to its mass, so I dug around in my junk drawer and found a rust-orange ribbon. I tucked it along the nape of my neck and pulled it up to corral my mass of curls back from my ears and off my face, in a kind of giant, loose, bell-shaped ponytail.

    Pretty Me entered the kitchen to grab some breakfast.
    Richie and Robbie were at the coffeemaker, filling large mugs with the bitter steaming brown liquid. They wore the same clothes they had on the night before, so they must have followed through on their vow not to sleep.
    When they saw me, they dashed, out passing Dad, who came in to refill his coffee cup, only to puzzle over the mere quarter-cup of dribble now remaining in the pot.
    I took my bowl of cereal and juice to the table and sat. Mom had her head buried in the Sunday paper, Dad returned to bury his in another part of the paper. Neither of them noticed the new, improved, prettier me, nor my tired, disheveled, and highly-caffeinated brothers.
    I ate my cereal quietly as Richie and Robbie gagged down sips of coffee. Robbie added more sugar to his, all the while staring intensely at me, making me feel self-conscious. I mean, yes, so I'd dressed a bit nicer than usual, but did Pretty Me look so different that he should stare at me this intensely?
    Soon both of my brothers stared at me in silence.
    Finishing my cereal, I very deliberately put my spoon down, set my face, narrowed my eyes, and stared

right back at them.

The game was on.

The three of us sat frozen, the *tick, tick, tick* of the wall clock measuring off how long we could keep it up.

Mom, finally aware of how unusually quiet my brothers were being, lowered her paper. She glanced askance at them to see them both staring hard at me.

Dad heard the rustle of Mom's paper. Curious, he lowered his too. He glanced at Mom, who was now staring at the boys, so he stared at the boys too, who were still both staring at me.

Mom and Dad turned their heads to look at me.

And now...*everyone* was staring at me.

I finally cracked, shaking off my stare.

I stood up, presenting myself as if on stage, extended my arms with a "ta-da" gesture, and announced, "**Fine!** If you all think I look so *stupid* in this, why don't you just *say so!*" before stomping out of the room in a huff.

I yanked the ribbon from my hair as I tromped upstairs. I locked my door, washed the makeup off my face, and changed into my usual overalls and tee. As I put the stupid Pretty Me clothes back in my closet, I looked at all Ronnie's things hanging there, and it got me thinking—if I couldn't be pretty on my own, I still had the world's best fallback position, no?

But that required the cassette tape. I dashed to the boys' room while they were still at breakfast and made a quick rifling of Robbie's toy chest to switch our mixed-up recordings back. I returned to my room to pick out one of Ronnie's most flattering outfits, folded it neatly, and loaded it into my backpack along with my Walkman and tape for school the next day.

The rest of the day I sat at my desk studying,

only emerging to grab a sandwich when I was sure no one else was in the kitchen. The family left me alone, which was welcome, but also disheartening.

Unable to shake my mood, I glanced over. That stupid poster on my wall about making lemonade mocked me from across the room, so I crossed to it, ripped it down, wadded it in a ball, and stuffed it in my trash bin, concluding that being required to make lemonade because you are constantly being pelted by lemons only succeeds in making one sour.

Not taking my invisibility completely for granted, I avoided all eye contact and conversation as I attended each of my morning classes—I even avoided raising my hand when no one else knew the answer. I kept an eye out for Bud. I was willing to talk if he was, but he wasn't in any of my morning classes and I didn't see him in the halls between. He basically knew my schedule, so I had to conclude he was deliberately avoiding me.

Lunch hour hit and I headed to my usual changing spot: girl's restroom at the far end of the mathematics wing. Wouldn't you know it, the moment I emerged from the bathroom as Ronnie, there was Bud, just down the hall from me.

Ronnie waved.

Okay, here we go.

Bud glanced at the floor and rubbed the back of his neck. After a moment's hesitation, he raised his head and approached. I watched his piqued expression slowly melt away as his eyes met Ronnie's.

"Hi, Bud," Ronnie perked.

"Hi. Gee, you look...*great*," Bud stammered out, once again done in by Ronnie's beauty. Yup—he simply glazed over, speechless, before mustering the strength to tear his eyes from her and stare at the floor again, I assume to re-muster the courage to confront her.

He took a breath and started speaking before looking up. "Ronnie, uh...why did you ditch me Saturday night?"

Ronnie rolled her eyes skyward before returning a sweet look at him. She reached out, took his face in her hands to secure his gaze, and mustered up a cute little pout for him.

"I'm sorry. I just...I *had* to go," she answered in a gentle tone topped with a few extra eyelash bats. "Do you *forgive me?*"

"Uh, *yeah*..." Bud sighed, glazing over again. "Sure. No problem."

And that was that.

I estimated for me and Bud to make up would take a few weeks of work at best. Ronnie managed to pull it off in mere seconds. And suddenly, I felt both angry and *very powerful.*

The next couple of weeks became a blur as I *fully* exploited the new power being Ronnie allowed me.

For example, I sat in the grass at lunch hour braiding a crown of daisies in order to then make Bud wear in front of everyone. There was a passive-aggressive hostility to some of the things I encouraged Ronnie do to Bud, the worst of which was to get him all ready to kiss her and then...make *sure she didn't.* For some reason Ronnie didn't fight me on this. Maybe being a tease was part of her innate personality?

I became Ronnie during Bud's football practices too, when the cheerleading squad wasn't in practice, knowing that sitting in the bleachers to watch them run plays would distract him and make him screw up more often. Ronnie blissfully played along—to her it was all sincere enthusiasm for the sport. For me, it was vengeful and yeah, ugly.

And I went to the mall as Ronnie with the popular girls rather than spend the time with Bud—another thing I found worked well to further torment him. Playing hard to get was natural for Ronnie, and it drove Bud *crazy*. At the time, I didn't stop to think how deliberately cruel I was being to him. In retrospect, sure, I knew it was, but then, I figured if Bud didn't want me, the *real* me, then he should have a dose of his own medicine—or something like that.

Bud had other problems too, because it was now all over the school that he was also dating the *real* me on the sly, not just Ronnie. Try as he might to shake the rumor mill, the snickers and whispers persisted, with his good buddy Durk making fun of him and pushing the story hard. And *I* did my best to keep the rumors going—by *categorically denying* to anyone who questioned me and would listen that Bud and I were *not* an item.

Wearing Ronnie's demeanor and trappings, walking her walk, actually **being** the most popular girl in school, was addictive. Not only was I no longer invisible, as Ronnie, I experienced visibility-plus. I commanded everyone's attention without even trying. It was a total rush to have every eye on me, every girl looking at me in either admiration or envy, every boy looking at me with desire, and **everyone** wanting to be my friend.

And since my brothers had decided I was some sort of *Body Snatchers* space alien mutant, they avoided me like the plague, which was an added plus. It seemed like my parents were avoiding me too, but it was hard to tell if it was avoidance or just Mom's book promotion deal sucking up all the oxygen in their parental bubble. At any rate, I was able to come and go at will without any interference—and what was wrong with *that?*

Of course, also thanks to Ronnie, my school work began to *very* seriously suffer. I had a speech due in English and had to completely ad lib it using blank note cards—sure, I had already had my topic in mind, the intelligence of dolphins, and had done a little research I was able to recall from memory, but had not really prepared at all. Fortunately, my impromptu performance was passable, considering, even down to my flipping through the blank cards to "find" a note or two, just to make it look legit, but I noticed that Mr. Toomey played with his mustache more than usual during my vamping and ultimately only gave me a B+.

And I actually played hooky for the first time in my life as Ronnie in order to go clothes shopping with the other popular girls, missing Ms. Lyle's afternoon AP Calculus class and further depleting my college fund. I wasn't yet sure how I'd explain away my absence. With a test coming up the following week I knew I was risking a lot—turned out the day I missed was the day she did test-prep.

When I finally took the test and got my first C ever, it was a *blaring* wake-up call.

Chapter Seventeen

SCARLET LETTER

Alone in Ms. Lyle's empty classroom, staring at my Calculus test paper with its big red "C" at the top, I thought of Hester Prynne—my scarlet letter of shame I would wear on my curriculum vitae rather than my clothing, but it was just as humiliating.

What have I done? I thought, forcing back tears. I put my head in my hands as I rewound my past few weeks of Ronnie revelry.

I was *completely* addicted to the power of being her.

As I lifted my head, a foot in my sightline next to my desk startled me. I jerked up to find Lainey standing there with Dinah at her side.

I wiped my eyes on my sleeve and snuffed, "I didn't hear you come in."

"You weren't supposed to."

Lainey grinned at me smugly.

"I was *right*, wasn't I? You *like* being her."

I spun the test paper around so it faced her, and pointed.

"This is my first C ever. I may have just screwed my perfect GPA."

"Seems a small price to pay—you got your boyfriend, *didn't you?*"

"I suppose," I mumbled back, then reconsidered. "*No*," I corrected, "*she* did. I'm just along for the ride."

"Sometimes the ride is all you get."

"I want off. Lainey, how do I get off?"

I started to blubber, "Okay! Yes! I like being

pretty, having everyone like me, having *Bud* like me... but...it's *cheating*, doing this. And every possible ultimate outcome I run in my head ends in disaster."

I dropped my head to the desk and went into a full sob.

"I...*deserve to fail.*"

I heard Lainey pull over a chair to face me. She waited patiently while Dinah stropped my leg until I was sobbed out. When I finally lifted my head, Lainey wore an uncharacteristic look of compassion. She opened her mouth to speak just as I felt my body spasm.

"Oh-no. What...time...is it?" I gasped.

Lainey stood and stepped back, watching me start to transform without answering.

Clinging to the edge of the desk, I glanced at the clock, as my breasts filled out and my waist cinched in with the now routine crunching of my pleasure/pain metamorphosis.

"Excuse me..." I wheezed between pangs, hearing my voice morph into Ronnie's as I did, "...it's practice time...."

Lainey mirrored my contortions of pain in her own face.

"...*help me, Lainey...please...*"

Then, Ronnie fully arrived, all grins and giggles. She stood and stretched, as if just up from a nap.

"Showtime! Where's the team?"

"On the field," Lainey rasped back to her. "Better run, you'll be late for practice."

At this point I was resigned to cede everything to Ronnie during cheerleading practice—I was clueless as to what to do anyway and preferred to passively brood about my C while she hopped and flipped and giggled around with her squad in time to their dumb, barely-rhyming chants.

Meanwhile in the center of the field, the football team began to assemble. I didn't see Bud there, but he soon emerged from the boy's locker room. Durk was right on his tail, saying something I couldn't completely hear, but it looked like Bud was annoyed by whatever it was Durk said.

As they drew nearer, I could just catch the rest of the conversation.

"I'm gonna ask Ronnie, okay?!" Bud snapped, at Durk, in an audibly loud whisper.

"Don't you mean Ron-***duh?*** Duh, as in the sound a *moron* makes when he asks a *dog* out on a date," Durk chided back, not making any effort to keep *his* voice down.

Bud turned back to face Durk down. Durk puffed himself up to his full head taller than Bud height, stuck his chin out, and smirked.

"Why are you being such an asshole?" Bud said, puffing himself up too.

The two stood there, chin to chin.

"*I'm* an asshole?" Durk countered with a sneer. "I'm not the one secretly dating the Eleanor Roosevelt clone."

Bud gave Durk a shove.

"Leave Rhonda out of this—she hasn't done anything to you!"

Bud was standing up for me? My ears perked up.

"I'm sorry. I forgot she's your *girlfriend*."

"She's ***not my girlfriend!***"

And there it was.

Bud shoved Durk again. Durk slugged him back and within seconds the two were brawling in earnest. The practice meet dissolved in an instant into chants of, "Fight! Fight! Fight!" A whistle trilled and Coach Ferguson charged over to the rumble just in time to keep them from killing each other.

"**BREAK IT UP!** Break it up, boys! Cut the crap right now—save it for the field!" he scolded, stepping in between them. "Any more out of either of you and there'll be a couple of warm spots on the bench this week the size of your asses!"

Bud and Durk got up and faced off. Durk snorted like a bull at Bud, turned, spat on the ground, and then ran out to join the other guys on the field. Coach Ferguson followed, but Bud lingered, with his hands on his knees, shaking his head and mumbling to himself.

"*C'mon, Langston!* **NOW!**" Coach Ferguson ordered.

Bud held up a finger to indicate he needed a minute. Then, he stood upright, marched over to me, gripped me by the shoulders, and said, in a very firm, forceful voice, "Would you like to go to the senior ball with me?"

"Sure," Ronnie squeaked back.

"**Good!**"

And with that, Bud turned and marched out to the field to join the others. Ronnie's squad tittered and clucked their social congratulations to her. My heart withered up inside while Ronnie's swelled with pride.

The next morning, in response to an official summons I received in first period, I knocked on the door to Ms. Swanson's office.

"Come in."

I peeked in the door.

"You wanted to see me?"

Ms. Swanson lowered the glasses on her nose to

look up at me, lips pursed. She waved me in.

"Close the door and have a seat, Rhonda."

I sat while Ms. Swanson opened a folder and flipped through the papers inside, shaking her head.

"Am I in some sort of trouble?" I asked.

"That's what I want to find out from you. I've received several...*uncharacteristic* memos concerning you over the past month. Starting with this one from Coach Tarbo about your involvement in a fight in the girl's locker room. Then there's this note from Nurse Weld claiming you faked an injury to get out of P.E." She held it up. "That was followed by a tardy slip." She held it up too, and then continued doing so with each of the rest of the memos, as if showing me court exhibits. "Another tardy, absent, tardy, tardy...."

She stopped on the next one, scanning it, and kinda huffed before holding it up.

"And here's a personal note to me, from Mr. Randall, wondering why I insisted he take you into his already full class when you are only doing average work."

"Randall's a jerk."

She dropped the note and pushed her glasses back up on her nose to look me straight in the eyes.

"Regardless of what you, *or I*, think of Mr. Randall, these grades he cites are *not* up to your capabilities."

There was a lingering pause. She was obviously waiting for me to say *something*, to offer *some* sort of explanation or excuse, but I shrugged instead.

Her stern approach not working, Ms. Swanson removed her glasses, rocked back in her chair, and reset her facial expression into one of sympathy.

She folded her hands on her desk and leaned forward again.

"Rhonda," she continued in a softer tone, "I *know* you. This isn't *you*. With the SAT's coming up next Saturday, you should be studying *more*, not *less*. Do you want to tell me what's going on?"

Ms. Swanson had always been super-kind to me and I liked her, so, yeah, I felt guilty sitting here, icing her out. I had always had the sense that she was a lot like me when she was my age, and that gave me the feeling that she *got* me more than most other adults. I would have loved nothing more than to spill everything about the bite and Ronnie and the whole bloody mess to her. But then, maybe because she *was* like me, I already knew telling her would do no good, for if *I* were *her*, I'd think my story *crazy*, and then would come the question of how to deal with an obviously deranged student.

No, rather than being a solution to my problem, telling her would multiply it. So, I determined that I had to remain mute and as facially inscrutable as possible.

Ms. Swanson lips tightened. She straightened up. Now she was angry.

"You had better get your life back together, young lady. I can't do it for you. It's entirely up to you. Whatever is going on with you, life *isn't* easy. Life *isn't* fair. Get used to it, *get over it*, and get *back to work*. Am I getting through?"

I remained a sphinx.

"May I go now?"

Ms. Swanson leaned back again and heaved a breath. She reached into her drawer to extract and stack a series of pamphlets. She handed them to me.

"Read *these*," she sighed, "Maybe one of them will help you more than I can."

I leafed them: "Family Problems," "Safe Sex," "Child Abuse," "Drugs and You," "Teenage and

Pregnant," and "Going Through Puberty."

"*Now* you may go."

Exasperated!
That was the only way to describe the feeling I had standing in the school corridor outside Ms. Swanson's office with my handful of trite advice pamphlets.

And—*surprise*—there was no "I Was A Teenage Cheerleader" pamphlet to offer a step by step solution to *my* problem.

As I headed to my locker, I passed Josephine Kent. Another invisible person, like me. I backed up and handed her the stack of pamphlets before striding off.

I opened my locker. There lay the Walkman and my daypack with Ronnie's clothes waiting inside. The temptation was great. I hesitated, grabbed my binder and chemistry text instead, closed my locker and headed for the Chem lab.

Every team in the Chem Lab was at their station and already working on the day's experiment when I sidled in next to Bud. Our instructor, Mr. Hulett, who was at his desk in the front of the class with his feet up, reading, glanced over the top of his size-twelves as I opened my notebook.

"Ah, Miss Glock. So good of you to join us," he smirked, as he reached over to his roll book to mark me tardy.

I didn't—*couldn't*—look at Bud. I glanced at the day's experiment handout, and the vials of chemicals and equipment set out for us: The Briggs-Rauscher Oscillating Color Change Reaction. I had already read the chapter prep on this—a chemical reaction that is supposed to cause striking color changes in the solution from amber to clear and then to blue as it oscillates between increases in iodide ions reacting to starch.

"Haven't seen you around much lately," Bud whispered.

"Haven't noticed you looking," I shot back as I measured out the potassium iodate and diluted it with water into the beaker marked "Solution A" as per Mr. Hulett's instructions.

Bud slid over a beaker he had already mixed marked "Solution B" and began diluting hydrogen peroxide in the "Solution C" beaker.

"Look," Bud whispered back, "I'm really sorry about the way I acted after the dance, but...you've at least *gotta* admit, the whole thing was pretty *weird*. I had no idea what was going on..."

He slid over Solution C.

"...I *still* don't."

After a pause, I glanced up at Bud. Seeing his sincere look of regret, I felt bad for him and a little guilty, because it all really *wasn't* his fault any more than it was mine, and since then I'd been using Ronnie to torture him. But at this point, what could I say to explain or make things right?

"Rhonda, say something. I'm sorry. I'll say it again: *I'm sorry!* Are you **ever** gonna forgive me?"

"I...*I forgive you*," I sighed back, "but that doesn't mean I still don't hurt. I need time to get over feeling like I have some kind of social disease around you and all your friends."

"I just want everything back to normal between us. I want to be able to talk to you again."

"Why don't you talk to Ronnie instead? Isn't she your new best friend?" I pouted back.

Bud inhaled, "You're jealous of *Ronnie?*

Rhonda, that's just...completely *stupid*. You two are so totally different. And, you and I have been friends, like, *forever*...since grade school! I...you and I, we just *get* each other, and I don't want to *lose* that, and Ronnie has nothing to do with *that*."

He glanced away, I think mostly in embarrassment.

"Look," he continued, "it's...it's just *different* with Ronnie. I know, I know, **I know**...we don't have a lot in common, but that's part of what makes her so...*interesting*."

It felt like he wasn't really convincing either of us.

"And, just because I'm dating *her* doesn't mean *we* can't still be friends...*does it?*"

"I wish she never existed," I mumbled under my breath.

"You blame *her* for the other night, don't you?"

"Yes," I replied, thinking it over. "Yes, I *do*."

"And you had no idea what you were getting into when you put on her clothes and got in my car in her place? Come off it, Rhonda! You're not stupid. You *have* to have been at least as responsible as *she* was."

I knew he was right but I tightened my lips in a scowl, and shook my head anyway.

"Why do you hate *her?*" Bud asked, honestly puzzled. "What's *she* ever done to *you*? She's just a *beautiful girl*...."

"**Exactly!**" I snapped, a little too loudly. Looking him in the eyes, I lowered my voice back to a still forceful whisper. "And we all know how friggin' important *that* is...don't we, Bud?"

A tear ran down my cheek. I wiped it away with my arm and scowled at him.

"Congratulations, by the way," I continued, "I'm

sure she'll be the prettiest girl at the senior ball. Of course, I'll never know—*no one* is gonna ask me to the ball, are *they?*"

Bud's lips tightened into a scowl to match mine. He turned, gathered up his books, and stomped out of the classroom.

Mr. Hulett glanced up from his book again.

"My!" he smirked, marking in his roll book again, "People do come and go so quickly here!"

I poured Solutions A, B, and finally C into the large beaker on the magnetic stirring plate and joined the rest of the class as we observed the eddies of our resultant mixtures dramatically change color, as if by magic, from amber to blue to clear to amber to blue to clear....

Chapter Eighteen

CRITICAL MASS

Dad's office was on what was commonly called, "Medical Row," a mini-mall of private doctors' offices and specialist clinics adjacent to Autumndale Memorial Hospital. I parked the car at the curb, steeled myself, and got out.

Dad's' office was set near the end of the line of various medical specialists' offices: OBGYN, ENT, INT, ORTHO, ENTERO. Dad's sign read, Dr. Roger Glock M.D., with the words COSMETIC & RECONSTRUCTIVE SURGERY in hand-lettered gold over black enamel shadow followed by the abbreviations ACS, ASPS, PSRC, AAPS, and ASAPS beneath.

I stuck my head in through the door to a waiting room decorated in soft earth tones and framed Impressionist pastoral scenes. His cotton candy haired receptionist who always smelled of peppermint looked up and smiled.

"Hi, Rhonda, how nice to see you."
"Hi, Lois. Is he with a patient?"
"No. In his sanctum. You can go right in."
"Thanks," I replied and rounded her desk to head down the corridor, past Examination Room 1. Dad's office door was a plain unmarked one sandwiched between it and Examination Room 2, so that he could access both rooms directly from it.

I gently knocked and entered to find him sifting through and marking a stack of his patients' records. This was Dad's private lair, not like the two other antiseptically clean, bright examination rooms adjacent to it. This small wood-paneled space was a clutter of plastic surgeon paraphernalia: plaster body part castings, before and after photo albums, and walls displaying his numerous academic credentials. He wore his white medical coat over his shirt and tie. He still had the cup I gave him for Christmas several years back that said "Doctor Dad" next to him on his desk.

Rim-lit by the afternoon sun's soft diagonal stripes slicing through his blinds and tracing across his desk, the whole tableau was like a Norman Rockwell painting of some doctorial ideal.

"Um, Dad…?"

He looked up and smiled, pleasantly surprised.

"Hey! Ron, honey…hi!"

"Lois said you weren't too busy and that I could come in."

"Just finishing up my paperwork for the day," he said, stacking the last of the folders into his out box. "What's up?"

"Uh…nothing.…"

Dad let my obvious lie sit there and didn't press while I wandered about the room fiddling with his things. He eventually ventured an educated guess.

"Your brothers giving you trouble again?"

"No," I laughed. "*Well*…no."

I poked around the room for a while more before finally settling in the armchair across from his desk.

"Dad?'

Yes."

"May I ask you a *serious* question?"

"Sure, honey."

"Do you think I'm…*pretty*?"

"No."

He leaned in, and smiled.

"I think you're *beautiful*."

I frowned back at him to let him know I was being *serious* serious.

"*Really*, Daddy. I want your *professional* opinion."

"Oh. I see."

Dad stood.

"Okay, then."

He took my hand, leading me into Examination Room 2 next door.

"Sit up here."

I sat in the chair and he pushed the pedal several times to raise me up into the harsh lights he had swung in closer and clicked on. But as soon our eyes met, I couldn't help it. I started to cry.

"Hey...wait a sec. *Hey*," Dad cooed, "Honey, wait...aw, come here." He hugged me to his chest as I wept. "What's wrong?"

"I'm *not* pretty...am I?" I blubbered.

He reached over to grab a wad of tissues from a box on his tool taboret, cradled my chin in his hand, and daubed my face dry. He sighed a smile at me.

"You really *want* my professional opinion?'

I nodded and steeled myself.

"You're still too young for surgery."

"Daddy!"

"It's true!"

"Stop avoiding my question! I need you to be *totally honest!*"

He nodded and put his face into its professional, no-nonsense gaze.

He examined my face front on, then in profile. He took a last look at the front again before letting go.

"Well, if you are going for purely classic feminine facial proportions, your nose could be shortened and thinned just a tad at the bridge. I might enhance your cheekbones a bit too, but quite honestly, honey, your face is already very well-proportioned. And *that's* my honest, professional opinion."

"Would it be...*hard* to fix those things?"

He pulled over a tall, rolling stool, sat on it, and took my hands in his, then looked me straight in the eyes.

"Ron, every single day people come through my door wanting something changed. I give a woman bigger breasts this week, another, smaller breasts the next. Some people want to look like, like...*anyone* but themselves, and some are chasing an ideal version of how they think they *need* to see themselves. And others, well...as the ideal of beauty changes, they want me to change their faces and bodies to match it."

He leaned in to kiss me on the forehead.

"But, *you*...?"

He glanced at the ceiling, thinking, then back at me with a kind of misty-eyed look.

"How can I make you see what *I* see? I've known this *lovely* face of yours all your life. It is, *by far*, one of my all-time favorite faces. And *I*, both privately *and* professionally, *wouldn't change a single thing*."

I got home armed with a new resolve: to just shut everything and everyone out but my SAT studies. No Ronnie, no worrying about my looks, no Bud, no parents, no brothers, no visibility to anyone. There were no games, rallies, or cheerleading practices between now and the test on Saturday morning—only the game later that Saturday night, but that gave me clear sailing at least until the test was done.

The first thing I did was to grab a big empty

cardboard box out of the garage and tote it up to my room. I emptied all Ronnie's clothes from my closet and dresser and piled them into it. I took an old empty shoebox rattling around in my closet and went to the bathroom, dumping all her cosmetics and such into that, and added it to the bigger box. I even threw in the cassette tape. Then I toted all of it down to put it in the side yard with the trash.

As I reentered the house, I spied Robbie observing me from around the corner of the kitchen doorway. I heard what must have been Richie rattling around in the kitchen, the sound of the sink faucet going on, followed by the disposal grinding away on something.

"What are you guys up to now?" I asked, then stopped myself, "Nope. Never mind—none of my beeswax."

As I headed for the stairs, I heard Richie say, "Robbie, get over here and dig out the next one."

"But I just saw Rhonda..."

Returning to my room, I locked my door and pulled out the four different SAT study guides from my bookcase I had accumulated, stacked them on the desk, and got to work.

I was so focused on my studies I had blocked out the repeated sound of the kitchen garbage disposal being run, and the sound of the front door opening and closing when Dad finally arrived home after picking up Mom. Mom's scream startled me out of my hyper-focused state, followed by a heated exchange between her and the brothers moving from the kitchen into the living room.

By the time I raced down the stairs to see what

the heck was going on, Richie and Robbie sat rigidly upright on the living room couch looking guilty while Mom stood before them seething, holding a large, green-glazed plant pot full of nothing but bare earth where her favorite fuchsia used to be.

Dad raced in from the garage. Mom held up the pot to show him as her anger melted into tears. She sobbed out, "They...down the *disposal...every* plant...my *fuchsia* was...about to *bloom*...."

Dad dashed over to wrap his arms around Mom and console her, making her sob even louder. He took the pot of bare earth from her and scowled at my brothers, setting his jaw.

Robbie glanced over at me, then back to Dad.

"But...it was full of pods!"

"Someday you'll *thank* us, Dad," Richie offered.

"I doubt that, Richard!" he snapped, and motioned for me to take the pot from him.

Both my brothers gave me the stink eye as I did.

"Can I **please** say something in our defense?" Richie continued.

Dad snapped up a stern hand to silence him.

"Richard, I wouldn't care if you brought in Will Robinson *and* his Robot to testify on your behalf. What you've done is **inexcusable!** You will **stop** playing these games. They have become **pathological!**

"There will be no more invasions, visitations, or transformations in this house!"

"Tell *her* that!" Robbie countered, pointing an accusatorial finger at me.

"**ROBERT!** I mean it! No more! You'll pay to replace every one of your mother's plants out of your allowance money. Now, apologize to her and then go to your room."

"Sorry, Mom," they both whimpered.

Mom sniffled and nodded in response.

As they passed me, Robbie stuck out his tongue at me and asked his older brother in a whisper, "*Now* what do we do?"

"We'll *prove* it," he whispered back, shooting me daggers.

Chapter Nineteen

R.I.P. S.A.T.

I was already seated on the school bus waiting to take us to Griffin High, where the SAT testing for the district was to be held, when Bud entered.

Ms. Swanson checked him off the list and nodded to the bus driver, "That's it."

The bus driver levered the door shut and started the bus.

Ms. Swanson turned to Bud, shaking her head at him.

"We just about left you behind, young man."

"Sorry I'm late," he apologized, as he scanned the bus for a seat. He took one up near the front right behind Ms. Swanson as the bus lurched into gear and started moving out of the Talbot High parking lot, but, glancing back and seeing me with an empty seat beside me, he carefully worked his way back to join me.

He sat and held out his SAT study guide.

"Quiz me?"

I looked at him and saw panic. Now was not the time to be anything but a supportive friend.

"Sure," I replied with an understanding smile, "You ready for this?"

"I don't know...I guess so? How about you?"

"I've been cramming all week. Actually, it's the first time in a while I feel prepared. Just had to keep all the distractions at bay, you know?"

Ms. Swanson, who had apparently been double-checking her list, stood up and called out, "Darleen Purdy? Is Darleen Purdy here?"

The freak who bit me?

About mid-bus, a hand went up. I scooted up in my seat to try to get a better look, but she was wearing a long coat, a hat, and sunglasses.

I had heard she was being home schooled, due to "emotional issues."

But I guess she still needed to show up to take the SAT—just my luck. Talk about distractions.

Darleen turned and lowered her sunglasses in order to look at me—I immediately slumped back down and looked away to avoid making eye contact.

I tried to shake it all off, and leafed Bud's test guide.

"Okay...let's run through some math questions. Ready?"

The testing was held in Griffin High's large conference hall, containing a sea of desks set up in pods of six with dividers between and around each individual desk to prevent copying. Each desk set-up included several number two pencils along with the test booklets and answer sheet, face down. There were several adult monitors, like Ms. Swanson, posted about the room and a test administrator, who introduced himself as Mr. Kahn, at the front.

Bud and I took seats in different pods far apart so as not to distract each other. It wouldn't have mattered to me. Nothing mattered or existed but the test—I was completely focused and ready.

I cleared my mind and took a few deliberately deep breaths while Mr. Kahn wound down his general instructions.

"...to ensure that you make maximum use of your time. At the conclusion of each testing period, a buzzer will sound...like *this!*"

A startlingly loud buzz echoed through the room, making all of us jump and a few people laugh.

"Before we begin section one, turn over and open your test booklets to page one and we will read the instructions together. **Do not** turn the page until you are instructed to do so."

I speed-read the entire instruction page while Mr. Kahn plodded methodically though it. I checked the points of my pencils to make sure none of them were loose. I scanned the answer sheet, with its little empty ovals I was eager to fill in—multiple choice, with a space for the essay. I should have been nervous, but I wasn't. I was excited. It had been a while since I was fully in my element. This was where I ruled, where I shone; this was my rally, my championship game, my book opening, my Olympics—my chance for gold.

Ugh, he's so slow—let's go, man!

Mr. Kahn couldn't talk any slower if he tried. I glanced at the clock—almost 9:30 AM. I unconsciously drummed my finger on the table top when the sound they made changed and I felt my fingernails begin to lengthen.

What the...?

I listened hard and could just pick up the faintest sound of Griffin High's marching band begin practicing out on their football field.

*No, no, no, n-n-nooo...! I don't **believe** this!*

I glanced about for a possible escape route, but there was none to be had and I was changing into Ronnie too fast, so I pulled my coat off of the back of my chair and wrapped it up over my head as I tried hard to suppress any of my or Ronnie's usual vocal grunts or giggles.

But I could do nothing to hide the wet, crunching

sounds of sinew and bone as I changed shape, and soon Mr. Kahn stopped droning mid-sentence.

"I heard other students mumbling too and then heard Mr. Kahn say, "Quiet please. Students, remain seated."

Shortly after that, my coat was pulled from my head.

Mr. Kahn looked down to see Ronnie smiling sweetly up at him.

"Young lady, what are you doing?"

"Nothing."

What was that crunching noise?"

He looked around the desk and floor, I presume to see if there were any candy wrappers.

She picked up a pencil and chewed on it, shrugging.

"We're about to begin the test."

"'Kay."

He put my jacket on the back of my chair for me and returned to the front of the room while Ronnie looked around and I went into a full-on, major-league freak-out inside her head.

*Ronnie, what the hell?! There's no **game!** No **rally!** No cheerleading practice! It's just a stupid band practice! And it's not even **our** band! Change back! **NOW!***

But if she heard me, she wasn't letting on. She actually seemed every bit as confused about this as I was, and it seemed as if the confusion made her more impervious to my influences than usual.

Mr. Kahn finished the instructions, concluding with, "You may now turn to page two and begin."

Holy...shoot! Okay, we can get through this— just do exactly what I tell you and we'll be fine. Are you listening to me?

Ronnie flipped the page and began reading the first question aloud.

"If car A travels at thirty miles per hour, and car B travels at..."

Several nearby students went, "Shhhh!" and one of the nearby monitors said, "Quiet, please. No talking!"

Ronnie clasped a hand over her mouth with a nervous giggle and looked around. That's when I caught a glimpse of Darleen sitting at the other end of the pod behind us, eyeing Ronnie.

Ronnie turned back to the test, tracing along the rest of the question with a pink fingernail as she continued reading.

She scratched her head, picked up a pencil, and glanced at the first row of empty ovals on the answer sheet.

It's B, Ronnie! The first answer is B! Fill in the B!

She sighed and shrugged.

"Eeny, meeny, miney, *mo*," she whispered to herself, and filled in the dot for D instead. Without going back to the test questions, Ronnie continued her rhyme, filling in more dots—then changed her approach, filling in the grid of little ovals to create the shapes of hearts, flowers, and happy faces while I hopelessly screamed, and screamed, and **screamed** at her inside her head, begging her to stop.

The wall clock read 12:30 PM when the band finally quit practicing and Mr. Kahn visited my desk to scold me again about my crunching noises, only to be confused seeing *me* hiding under my jacket instead of Ronnie. Once he finally moved on, I was poised to go at my answer sheets full of Ronnie's pointillist hearts, flowers, and smiley faces with the eraser end of a pencil when that ear-piercing buzzer went off, causing gasped startles and laughter again from everyone other than me.

I'm not sure how long I'd been sitting there, staring off into my own internal nothingness. I still felt as completely incapacitated as the experience of being inside Ronnie was during the test, but she was gone and now, *no one* was in charge. I honestly don't even remember leaving the Griffin High conference room, or getting back on the bus, or any of the trip back to Talbot High. My mind held only the scorched-in after-image of my completely screwed-up answer sheet full of Ronnie's idiotic half-erased daisies and hearts and that shrill sound of the buzzer going off, ending my life.

"C'mon, kids! I haven't got all day," Lenny, our bus driver, hollered back through the empty bus, forcing me out of my stupor.

"Lighten up, will ya?" Bud protested back. He took my arm and helped me to a stand.

"Come on, Ron. We need to get off now."

We were off the bus.

The bus left.

Other than the two of us, the school parking lot was deserted.

I finally glanced at Bud.

He returned a sympathetic smile, put his arm around my shoulder, and led me to the curb, where we sat. He hugged me to his chest when I began to weep again.

"Hey, don't be so hard on yourself," he softly reassured. "You just had an off day. Happens all the time in football. It's not as bad as it feels right now. Tomorrow comes, and it's a whole new game. And if you really have to, you can always retake the test."

"Thanks, coach," I grumbled.

"I'm just trying to help."

"Look. I blew the test, Bud—*completely* blew it. That's it. My life is *over*. All my years of work led to...*nothing*. I got...*nothing*."

"You've always got me."

I looked at him. He shot me back a misty-eyed half-smile.

I *sooo* needed to believe him, more than ever before. And I wanted to believe him so badly that I would have willingly failed a dozen SATs just to hear him say what he said again, if I knew he meant it the way I wanted him to.

"Right," I heard myself mumble back.

I inhaled a deep, staccato breath, wiped my eyes dry with my sleeve, and stood.

"Thanks, Bud, really—*thank you* for staying here with me," I added. "I'll be okay now."

I glanced over at the family car.

"I'd better get home."

I was greeted by an envelope taped to the front door with my name on it. The note inside read:

> Rhonda,
>   Your father and I are in Cleveland for the book fair. We'll be home late tomorrow. There's a casserole for dinner in the fridge. You're in charge so don't let your brothers do anything crazy.
>   Love,
>   Mom

I entered the house with a sigh.

"Richie! Robbie! I'm home!"

The house was as quiet as a tomb, which should have made alarms go off in my head, but I was too emotionally exhausted to care. Instead, as I slogged up the stairs, I listed the most extreme things I could imagine those brats doing and *still* not care: running away from home to join the circus, setting fire to the town hall, setting fire to themselves...

Now there's an idea.

What the...?

The door to my room was ajar.

I pushed it wide open. My room was pitch-dark inside. I stepped in, clicked on the ceiling light, and stopped dead.

My bedroom was completely empty, save the box of Ronnie's stuff I'd thrown away now sitting in the middle of the floor. It was dark because my window had been boarded up from the outside.

"What the...?"

Not really believing my eyes, I instinctually crossed to the window to confirm what I was seeing. When I did, the door behind me clicked closed, and as I spun back, I saw the rod of the doorknob slip out through its now-empty hole.

I dashed over to try to open it as I heard metal bolts click shut from the outside. I peeked through the empty knob hole to see my brothers staring back from the other side.

"You guys are in **WAY** big trouble! Open this door...**NOW!**

A note slid in under the door:

Not until you tell us the TRUTH!

"Truth?! About *what?* Richie, answer me! You two are gonna get **killed** when I tell Mom & Dad about this!"

Another note:

> Remember— we saw you mutate.

I picked up the note and stared at it, collapsing to the floor with my back against the door. My mind logged this apt metaphor of my life: an empty room with only a box of Ronnie's stuff sitting in the middle of it. How had it all gone so wrong?

I was numb.

Another note slid under the door:

> Tell us all.

A microphone poked through the hole where the knob had been and snaked down on its wire to rest on the floor beside me. I started to laugh in frustrated hysteria.

"If I told you guys the truth, you wouldn't believe me."

After a pause, another note:

> Yes we would.

Maybe they would...

"Okay, I'll tell you guys what happened, but you *gotta* keep it a secret."

> Face the camera.

I turned to look through the knob hole again. Richie had Dad's video camera's lens poked into it, filming me.

"Hey—you can't show this to anyone! Turn it

off! I mean it!

I could hear the camera running.

"Fine, then. You win. I'll tell you the truth...but then you have to let me out."

I sat facing the knob hole, took a breath, and launched in:

"So, this weird old lady, or maybe she's a witch...? I don't even really know...she's the janitor. Anyway, she wrote this spell...well, she *wasn't* old or a janitor when she *wrote* it, she was my age. It was a long time ago. It was supposed to make her the most beautiful cheerleader in the school so this football player guy would like her. Anyway, her spell worked until she got mad and bit another girl.

"This is sounding *sooo* **stupid**.

"Well, when she bit the other girl, *that* girl changed into a cheerleader instead of her. And then *that girl* bit someone else and so on. Anyway, I got bit by this insane little idiot, Darleen Purdy, and now every time there's a football game or rally or whatever, I change into a cheerleader.

"That's the God's-honest truth. That's it."

I heard the camera click off. There was a long pause, then another note:

We don't believe you.

"*Wha...?!* But it's the **truth!** I swear to *God* you guys! Please! Let me out and I can *prove* it!"

I approached the knob hole and spoke more softly through it, pleading.

"Robbie, honey...*you* believe your big sister, don't you?'

I looked down, hoping to see another note.
None came.

I collapsed to my knees and pounded on the door.

"C'mon, you guys! **Please** let me out!"

Chapter Twenty

ALL THE WORLD'S A CAGE

The afternoon ticked on. I tried dislodging the pins from the door hinges and fiddled with what remained of the latch inside the knob hole, but without anything left in my room to pry or bang at either of them, it was no use. I searched the box of Ronnie's stuff, hoping to find something to use as a tool, but there was nothing in there either. It sounded like they added dead bolts to the outside of my door anyway, in case I removed the pins.

My brothers may have been crazy, but they weren't stupid.

I examined the window next. They'd nailed boards over it from the outside, so I couldn't even crank open the casement in order to give a whack at trying to loosen them. I squinted through a crack between the boards at the setting sun.

They eventually slid a couple of peanut butter and jelly sandwiches wrapped up in saran wrap under the door—it looked like they'd flattened them with a rolling pin in order to make them fit, but I didn't care because it must have been around dinner time and I was starving. Apparently, they couldn't figure out a way to get me anything to drink with it. Eating a PB&J without anything to wash it down was annoying, so I went in and drank from my bathroom faucet—in the process I managed to get one side of my hair sopping wet. There was no towel, of course, so I stood over the sink trying to wring it out as much as I could.

I'd never wanted to kill my brothers more than

at that very moment.

I scoured the bathroom, looked in the medicine cabinet, in the cupboard, then under the sink. The brats had picked those clean of everything too.

Jeez.

They must have been planning this whole thing for a while and then spent the whole morning moving things out while the folks were off to Cleveland and I was off taking, *correction*...watching Ronnie **screw up** my test.

I was just about to climb under the sink to see if I could dislodge the plunger mechanism or some other mechanical part down there to use as a prying tool when I felt the now all-to-familiar jolt of pleasure/pain that had become so routine.

Oh, no! I totally forgot. Tonight's game must be starting.

I staggered back into my room and sat on the floor next to Ronnie's box of stuff awaiting her arrival. I glanced over to see the camera lens aimed through the knob hole again as all the bone-crunching started and Ronnie emerged.

I woke up stiff from sleeping on the floor. Ronnie's prom dress was wadded up under my head for a pillow with the prom dress she'd bought for me acting as my blanket. I sat up and looked around at the aftermath of Ronnie's one-person slumber party. She'd emptied the contents of her box of stuff all across the floor, including her box of make-up. It was then I remembered my toenails were now painted pink.

My mouth was dry and mucky from not being able to brush my teeth the night before, so I staggered into the bathroom. That's when I saw my reflection and realized I was wearing her damned cheerleader outfit, with a scrunchie in my hair, high up on the crown of my head—my own hair's transition back had replaced her cute ponytail with a rust-red pom-pom ball of my own frizz that listed to the left.

I moaned as I pulled the scrunchie along with several of my hairs loose.

I rinsed my mouth and splashed some water on my face before recalling I had no towel. I staggered back to the bedroom and used one of Ronnie's tee shirts to dry off. I tossed it in the box. I changed back into my own clothes and began tossing all Ronnie's stuff back into the box too. That's when I finally noticed that another note had apparently been slipped under the door while I was sleeping.

I crossed to it and read:

Now <u>EVERYONE</u> will believe us!

I moaned again—and started pounding on the door.

"Okay! You have your evidence now! So, let me out! C'mon, guys! I want my stuff back. I'm hungry—I want breakfast. You ***win*** okay?! Just open the door!"

I heard the doorbell ring, so I started yelling as loud as I could.

"HELP ME! I'M TRAPPED UPSTAIRS! WHOEVER YOU ARE—*PLEASE,* **HELP*!*"**

I heard the front door opening and my brother's voices arguing with a woman's voice I didn't immediately recognize.

"HELP ME! *UP HERE!* **HELP ME!**" I screamed louder.

Soon there were heavy footfalls on the stairs coupled with my brothers' protestations while the deadbolts snapped loose and the door opened.

There stood Lainey, with a squirming brother on each arm, trying to hold her back, while Dinah tugged and snarled at Richie's pant leg.

"*Rigescunt indutae!*" Lainey commanded. Nothing happened, the boys kept up their squirming. Lainey swore, "Damn, these old Latin spells never work for me." She screwed up her face and chanted more firmly:

"*Brothers freeze
Until I please!*"

Both boys flew off of her and froze in rigid, spell induced paralyses.

Lainey looked at me. "How in the **world** do you put up with these two?!"

"It isn't easy. Thank God you're here—but how did you know?"

"Last night's game was, *ehem*...short a cheerleader."

"But, how did you find me?"

She jingled her wad of keys and smiled.

"Office records," she explained. "But that's not why I'm here."

She removed a tote bag from her shoulder and set it on the floor next to her.

"I think I can solve your little problem—or at least there's a *chance* to set things right."

She turned and addressed my immobilized brothers.

"I'm your sister's friend. You two have a decision to make. Do you want me to be your friend too, or an enemy? Keep in mind, I make a very powerful enemy."

My brothers listened and blinked and took it all in.

"I'll release you now—*if* you promise to behave.

Blink twice if you want to be friends and promise to do as I say."

They both double-blinked several times through panic-stricken eyes.

*"For both not one:
My spell be done!"*

Richie and Robbie jerked free with loud, *Aaak*s, causing Robbie to trip over Lainey's tote. Some of its contents tumbled out across the hallway floor. Among jars and pouches of what looked to be weird things like dried frog's legs, bat's wings, and oddly-shaped roots, a shrunken head rolled across the floor and spun to a stop next to Richie's foot.

Instead of screaming, as someone *normal* might, Richie picked it up and examined it, fascinated.

"Cool," he decided.

Robbie sidled over to admire it too. It was soon obvious, by his crestfallen look, that he was disappointed with not having one of his own.

Lainey reached into her bag and pulled out a small stuffed alligator. She handed it to an immediately delighted Robbie.

"You two can keep those...since were all friends now. But only *if* you behave and stop tormenting your sister," Lainey offered.

They looked at their things, then at me, then Lainey, then me again.

"Are you the one who made her change?" Robbie asked.

"Not on purpose."

"I **told** you it was the truth," I stated, crossing my arms in an air of vindication. "**Now** do you believe me?"

They looked at their things, then at me, then Lainey, then me again, and nodded.

"How long will it take you to put your sister's room back the way you found it?" Lainey posed.

Richie thought for a second.

"Twenty-seven minutes."

"We have a system," Robbie added.

"Good then," Lainey continued. "We'll see you in the kitchen when you're finished."

I made Lainey some tea and toast while I scarfed down Richie and Robbie's leftover cold casserole and a couple of pop tarts. By the time I felt sated, my brothers arrived to announce that my room was put back as they found it.

Richie still had Dad's video camera and was taping Lainey and narrating.

"Our story takes on a new twist with the arrival of...."

He stopped taping.

"Excuse me...what's your name?"

"You may call me Ms. Moody," she replied.

"Um...you don't mind them taping you?" I asked, hoping she would.

"Not in the least," she replied with a wink and a smile. "Well, boys, let's get started," she continued, standing and taking her tote to the kitchen counter. "You," she pointed to Robbie, "pull over that step stool so you can help me."

Robbie obliged and was soon carefully measuring out and handing Lainey various odd ingredients, which she pinched, spooned, or poured into the Cuisinart. Its contents soon roiled and began to steam. Lainey turned to Richie.

"Now, where's that shrunken head of yours?" Lainey asked.

Richie set down the camera and raced upstairs and back in record time, handing it to her.

Lainey plucked a hair from it, dropping it into the Cuisinart too. She tossed the shrunken head back to Richie, put the lid on the Cuisinart, and pureed the concoction into a green-gray glop. She stopped the machine, remembering something, and in a quick snap of her wrist, plucked out several of my hairs.

"Ow!" I mewled.

"Don't be such a baby," she cackled back, as my brothers snickered along with her.

She whirred my hair into the glop for a while longer while chanting, "*Nolite primam mutationem in osculo sancto.*"

She looked into the Cuisinart, smiling, as the concoction burped.

"Huh. The Latin actually worked this time."

She removed the container from the Cuisinart and poured its contents into a Pyrex glass loaf pan, then placed the pan into the microwave.

"Oh!" she exclaimed, looking at Richie again, "I almost forgot the final ingredient. Here, hand me the camera—I don't want you to miss this."

Richie reluctantly handed the video camera to Lainey, who popped it open, took out the cassette, tossed it into the glop, and started the microwave.

"Hey!" he protested.

"Shhh!" Lainey scolded, then chanted, "*Dianae facere ius!*"

There was the sound of a muted explosion in the microwave—when Lainey finally opened it, its inside walls were speckled in the now-glowing glop.

"You'll want to clean that out right away," she

warned, so I grabbed a dishrag, wet it, and began cleaning while she extracted the now partially-melted videotape and dumped it into the trash bin.

She poured the glop into a juice glass and set the Pyrex loaf pan into the sink, rinsing it clean with warm soap and water.

The glowing glass of gray-green glop had faded and stopped burbling and steaming by the time she handed it to me with the command, "Drink it."

"*Really...?*" I grimaced back.

"Really!"

Before I could allow myself to think about how stupid it was to do so, I pinched my nose and gulped the glop down without stopping until the glass was emptied.

If, as the nursery rhyme claims, girls are made of "sugar and spice and everything nice," this concoction was that poem's polar opposite. I fought my automatic gag response, figuring it would do me no good to barf it all back up. When my nausea mellowed, I glanced at my brothers, who actually looked so impressed and proud of me for drinking the gunk and holding it down that I thought I might just love them after all.

Lainey soaped and rinsed the glass.

Would it be okay," I wheezed, "I mean, can I rinse my mouth and drink some water?"

"Oh, sure," Lainey tossed back, "It's done doing whatever its going to do, if it is going to do anything."

Richie dug in the trash, extracting the ruined videotape, being careful not to get any of the glop on his hand.

"It's toast," he complained.

You wanna do magic, you gotta pay the price," Lainey chuckled back.

"This isn't some monster movie, Richie," I

added, "It's my life."

'What's the difference?" Robbie snarked.

I had no snappy comeback.

I turned to Lainey.

"You mean…it's over now? No more Ronnie?" I asked, almost daring to smile.

"Oh, no, nothing of the sort," she explained, as my heart sank. "I only *altered* the spell. To actually break it you have to be kissed by the light of a full moon, by your one true love. Until then, everything stays the same."

"True love's kiss?" Richie smirked.

Robbie started making kissy noises and moaning, "Oooh, Prince Charming, you're so alarming. Ooooh. Kiss me."

Lainey crossed to the table to pick up Richie's shrunken head. She dangled it in front of his eyes by its hair.

"As for you, mister smart-mouth, if you say anything more about any of this to anyone, or mistreat your sister again, *this* will be you. Got it?"

Richie gulped and nodded mutely.

She glanced at Robbie, who also nodded like a bobble-head.

Chapter Twenty-one

EXTREME MAKEOVER

Once Lainey left, I went up to inspect my room with Richie and Robbie following behind. Miraculously, and true to their word, my brothers had replaced everything so perfectly that it felt as if none of the past 17 hours had ever happened. I breathed a big sigh of relief.

"You know, you guys may be annoying, but you *do* have your moments."

"Sorry we didn't believe you," Robbie offered.

"Yeah, sorry," Richie added.

The three of us looked at each other and before we could allow ourselves to feel awkward about it, we were engaged in a group hug.

Richie pulled free first, pondering aloud, "When's the next full moon?"

I crossed to my desk area by the window to look at my wall calendar, but it was missing.

"Oh! Sorry, sorry, *sorry*...!" Robbie repeated as he dashed out of the room to return a moment later with the calendar and a push pin.

He pinned it up and the three of us scanned it.

"Tonight?" Richie and I said in unison, as we eyed today's square, the same square in which I had months earlier written and circled, "Senior Prom Nite."

"What are you gonna do?" Richie asked.

My mind reeled through about a dozen different scenarios, editing and amending and combining each to come up with my one best possible approach.

"I...have an idea," I replied. "But I'll need your

help."

The brothers looked at each other, then back at me. Robbie shrugged, as if to say, "Why not?" but Richie looked to be rolling around his own list of scenarios in his head before he finally answered, "Okay, let's make a deal."

After a much-needed shower and some fresh clothes, the three of us jumped into the family car for a trip to the local nursery. The first part of Richie's deal was for me to help them replace all of Mom's plants they had pulverized—they used what they had of their allowance money and I was to pony up the rest. I suggested we throw in an extra African violet that was in full bloom, to offer her as an apology gift from them.

Okay, so I was in a generous mood—my brothers and I had been at odds lately, but the experience of actually enjoying doing something with them and having *someone* believe me and be on my side for once made me feel more family-oriented in general. And that started me thinking about Mom. I mean, Mom can't help being Mom any more than Ronnie can help being Ronnie, or I can help being me. I resolved to behave more magnanimously toward her too.

The second part of the deal—I ordered us a pizza when we got home. After we gorged on that, the three of us spent a couple of hours re-potting and restoring Mom's plants exactly as they once were. I tied a ribbon around the new African violet's pot and Robbie drew a "sorry" card for the two of them to sign and leave on the kitchen table next to the pot.

Then we tidied up and cleaned the house from top to bottom.

It was mid-afternoon when I finally started

collecting the return on our deal. Richie brought out their stash of hidden **National Enquirers** and we scoured all the red-carpet photos and make-over articles together, pulling out any useful make up tips and possible hairstyles.

"I like this one," I commented, pointing to something they had called a 'braided prom twist.'

The boys studied it.

"Can you pull it off?" I asked.

"We'll need to use some of Mom's hair products and curling iron, but sure," Richie replied, with a nod. "And you're gonna have to use a *lot* of conditioner."

While I took my second shower of the day, conditioning the hell out of my hair and scrubbing away any lingering potting soil from my nails, Richie set up a make-shift salon in their bathroom, where he went to work taming my tresses. I had to stifle a laugh, because he took it all *so seriously*—he had the picture and instructions taped to the mirror and all Mom's hair pins, gels, and sprays at hand. He stopped periodically to stoop in front of me, hands on knees, and stare at my head, then shake his head and go back at it. When he finally said, "There," and rotated the desk chair, and I saw his work, I stopped snickering.

The shape, shine, and styling were utter perfection! I turned my head from side to side, then grabbed up a hand mirror to more fully view the artfully intertwined plait of hair gracefully arcing from the back of my neck to be invisibly pinned to the top of my head.

"Richie, you're a genius."

Meanwhile, Robbie was off carefully ironing my prom dress—the one Ronnie bought me—so each pleat was crisp and in place. He even picked out a pair of

Mom's dress shoes that went well with the dress, and with a couple of cotton balls in each toe, I was all set.

"Hurry up! Let's see!" Robbie hollered from downstairs.

I looked myself over in my bedroom mirror.

Having done my best to follow the make-up instructions from various reference photos taped to my mirror and what little I remembered from Ronnie's make-up techniques, I had been able to create a very natural feel. The dress fit me like a glove, and with Richie's hair styling, I had to hold back tears, because I looked like some a kind of amazing idealized version of myself—but it *really was* me, just a me I never really knew was ever possible for me to be.

I descended the stairs with the soft rustle of tulle as Richie clapped and Robbie hammed a swoon from the foyer below.

I laughed.

"You look **great**, Sis," Richie admitted, sounding a bit proud.

"Thanks to **you guys**. My hair is just too amazing, Richie. The dress and shoes are perfect."

I did a spin to feel the flow of the dress follow after me.

Robbie dashed from the room and returned with something behind his back. He crossed to me and handed me a clear plastic box. Inside was a peach-colored orchid corsage.

"We got this for you at the flower shop—for luck," he explained.

"Oh, Robbie, Richie. I'll never forget this, you guys. **Never**."

"Just go break the spell. That Ronnie chick's too creepy," Richie laughed.

There was a moment of awkward silence that was broken by the sound of keys in the door, followed by Mom and Dad bursting in.

"We left early because my books sold ou..." Mom announced, stopping mid-sentence when she saw me.

Our eyes met and I could see tears well in hers. I felt tears well in my own. She crossed to me and took my hands in hers.

"It's prom night," I explained. "I wasn't asked, but thought I'd go anyway."

"Well, you look absolutely *beautiful*," Mom gushed, turning to Dad. "Doesn't she look beautiful?"

"If you want my professional opinion," Dad replied, winking at me, "I agree."

"**Wait!**" Mom squealed, making everyone jump. "Stay right here. Don't move."

She dashed up the stairs to their bedroom in a flutter, while the rest of us stood in in the hallway.

"Did the boys give you any trouble?" Dad asked.

"Nope. They were great," I replied.

"Nothing *unusual* happened?" he questioned, skeptically.

"Nope," Richie replied.

"Nope," Robbie repeated.

Dad eyed me in disbelief, but I simply shrugged. He wandered over to scrutinize Richie and Robbie, looking for hints that might betray that they were lying. He glanced past them, into and around the neat-as-a-pin house. He couldn't read them as well as I could—noting their buried conspiratorial smirks, my prediction was that they were now on to a new, novel, and completely unexpected way to torment the folks—by being uncharacteristically well-behaved.

I stifled a grin.

"May I please be excused now," Richie asked. "I have to do my homework."

"And I need to clean up my toys," Robbie added.

Mom burst out of their bedroom, giddy.

"Hold that thought," Dad told the boys.

She dashed back down the stairs to hand me a large, flat, antique blue velvet box. I opened it to reveal a stunning Victorian-era jewelry set.

"You don't *have* to wear these if you don't want to, but the colors are so *perfect* with your dress," Mom explained. "They belonged to your great-grandmother—they're set with peach moonstones and agates. I was saving this for your graduation gift. Now is better though, don't you think?"

"*Moonstones*," Robbie whispered. Richie nudged him quiet.

"They're *incredible*," I replied, picking up a brooch atop a comb, "but how do I..."

"Here, let me," Mom offered, taking the comb and carefully placing it into my hair just in front of my up-do plaits, as Richie cringed. She then helped me with the necklace, bracelet clasp, and earrings.

"The boys who didn't ask you will be kicking themselves tonight," Dad predicted.

"That's the idea," Robbie mumbled under his breath and to no one in particular. Richie nudged him quiet again.

"Well, I'd better go," I sighed, suddenly feeling nervous about the whole thing. "The dance started almost an hour ago."

"Let me drop you," Dad offered, holding the door open for me.

I turned back to look at Mom daubing at her running mascara with a tissue, her lower lip in a slight, quivering pout. Her look was uncharacteristically insecure; insecure on my behalf. She was worried about me, worried that I might get my feelings hurt, be disappointed, or mistreated.

Maybe she wasn't as bad a mom as I thought she was after all?

I found myself crossing to her and hugging her close for a moment. She leaned in and kissed me on the cheek.

"Good luck tonight, honey," she whispered, with a wink.

"Thanks, Mom," I replied, as I followed Dad out the door, whispering to myself, *"I'll need all the luck I can get."*

Chapter Twenty-two

THIS BUD'S FOR YOU

In front of the school, we could hear the music from the dance playing in the distance. Dad shot me a smile, leaned over, and kissed me on the cheek.

"For luck. And I bet I won't be the only one tonight."

"God, I hope not."

"Huh?'

"I'd...better go."

I carefully extracted my big-dress-clad self from the passenger seat, closed the door, and waved goodbye as Dad pulled away. Since the dance had been going a while the lot was full of cars but otherwise deserted. I glanced up at the night sky to confirm the moon was indeed full, but it was obscured by clouds. My mind recalled drinking Lainey's disgusting potion and I felt a touch of nausea at the memory of it—or it could have been nerves.

This all better work.

I turned and headed toward the dance. I wasn't used to walking in Mom's heels—it made me feel taller though and, as silly as it sounds, more like an adult. As I rounded the corner, I saw Bud sitting alone on the bench outside. I retreated a bit to duck behind a bush and figure out just how to approach the situation. It was fortuitous, him sitting there—*maybe this will be simpler than I thought.*

The moonglow increased around me and I looked up to see the clouds pull apart, exposing a very bright, full orb, which, when its light hit me, was immediately coupled with an unfortunately-timed jolt of pleasure/pain.

*What the...no, no, **no**...!*

A hand touched my shoulder, making me jump out of my morphing skin. It was Lainey with Dinah circling her feet.

"I forgot to tell you, the altered spell will be very... *unstable* in full moonlight," she whispered. She then noticed I was changing, "Oh, you already discovered it."

"Yeah, thanks for letting me know," I snarked back, then giggled insipidly, as Ronnie began to take over.

Bud must have heard our whispers and her giggles for, before I knew it, Lainey and Dinah had mysteriously vanished and he tucked himself into the bushes next to Ronnie.

"Ronnie?" he asked, sounding slightly annoyed. "What are you doing hiding in the bushes? You were supposed to meet me over an hour ago."

I saw his eyes quickly assess her—Ronnie didn't fit my dress well: the waist was loose and too high on her, and her added height made the length of the dress too short. The worst part though was I could feel her ampler bust doing a kind of tacky muffin-top at the bodice. Bud tried to hide his reaction to it all, but I could tell by the slight crease between his brows that he was a bit surprised by how uncharacteristically ill-dressed she was.

I cringed a bit at the thought of Richie's beautiful hairdo and what her hair may have just done to it.

Ronnie was oblivious to it all, of course, and simply perked, "Don't you look handsome!" back to him.

She took his arm and gave him a bubbly grin.

"Well, come on then. We're late as it is," he sighed, and escorted her out of the bushes and to the door.

I heard another rustle in the bushes on the other side of the path, coupled with a feeling that we were being watched and followed, but unfortunately Ronnie was solidly in control so I couldn't make her look back to check it out. It must have been Lainey and Dinah, but for some reason it made me uneasy anyway.

We stepped through the entryway into the huge darkened room. A sign made of twinkle lights on the far wall proclaimed "One Magic Night." The room was done up with full-sized trees draped with Spanish moss and more twinkle lights. Lanterns were strung between the trees with tables and chairs encircling the dance floor. From the ceiling they had hung a single large ball lamp, transparently painted to resemble a full moon. The whole tableau was actually pretty cool—like a nighttime park set in a bayou.

"Neat!" Ronnie exclaimed.

Bud gave her a second look, smiled a bit more hopefully, and said, "Now that you're here, I'm glad. Come on, let's dance."

But right as he said it, I could feel myself twitch and start changing back—I deduced that the clouds must be covering the moon again. I now had enough control coming back to be able to turn Ronnie's head and look back at the doorway. The dimming moonlight silhouetted an eerily-caped and hooded figure standing in it.

"Excuse me a minute," I said, abandoning Bud to dash for the ladies' room without taking the time for a response or to wonder who the weird figure in the doorway could be.

When I emerged from the toilet stall as myself again, I went to check my hair right off.

I let out a sigh of relief. Almost miraculously, the transformation to Ronnie's tresses and back had only loosened a few hairpins a bit and I was able to carefully push those back in place. Thankfully, Richie had used a **lot** of holding product. As I nudged the last pin back in place, I saw the reflection of the hooded figure enter the restroom and latch the door behind her.

I spun to face her. She lowered her hood.

It was an ordinary-looking girl my own age. I'd never seen her before, as far as I knew. But she looked at me as if *she* knew *me* well.

"Can I...help you with something?" I asked cautiously.

"Don't you recognize me?" she asked, pacing closer as I backed away.

"Not really," I replied sidling further away. "Should I?"

The strange girl kept approaching me. She smiled and recited, almost as if in a trance:

> *"Every girl who's pure of heart,*
> *Is pretty, clean, and neat,*
> *May be a member of the squad,*
> *If these four rules she'll meet:*
>
> *"She must be cute,*
> *She must have spirit,*
> *And sports must be her God.*
> *She mustn't ever fail a class,*
> *Or she'll be off the squad."*

"Darleen Purdy?" I asked. "You're the girl who... bit me?"

She nodded, inching closer still.

"This is what you did to me," she replied. "You ruined my life...***twice***. Now you have to fix it."

"Um...and how am I supposed to do *that*?" I asked, puzzled.

"***Bite me!***" she demanded, thrusting out her bare arm. "Do it! You don't want to be a cheerleader—I do! Give it back!"

Fortunately, my sidling around the room and inching away now had me close enough to the door to quickly unlatch it and make my escape without her grabbing my arm this time. Also, fortunately, outside the door a line of anxious girls waiting to pee blocked Darleen from following as I quickly 'scuse-me'd my way off into the crowded room.

I circled the dance floor. The first thing I noticed was everyone looked right at me. Some pointed and whispered to each other about me. Even Durk and Lydia gave me the once-over—I never expected to be noticed like this.

Huh.

And that's when it hit me—***I wasn't invisible anymore***. There was no more need for a fantasy me hidden inside. I hadn't yet broken the spell to be forever rid of the me that was Ronnie—but somehow, through the help of my brothers and my determination to finally step out of the shadows, to risk *wanting* to be seen by my peers, my inner conflict, my hidden parts, that feeling of invisibility had all vanished. I truly had become completely visible, which made me smile and boosted my confidence a bit.

Now, to find out if Bud sees me too.

I finally spotted Bud over by the punch bowl, sipping at a plastic cup and looking dejected. I approached him as casually as I could.

He saw me too—and in the way I'd been hoping for. His eyes took me in in a wide-open, stunned sort of way.

"Rhonda, hey," he smiled out. "Wow. I mean, *wow!* You look...amazing! For a second I thought you were...someone else."

"Yeah, wouldn't you know it...Ronnie wore the same dress," I deliberately overplayed for effect, trying to cover for the obvious, "I mean...*hello!* The 'ultimate prom nightmare'," I finished, with air-quotes.

"Looks better on you," Bud said with a kind of puppy-eyed and apologetic sincerity.

"Believe it or not, my brothers were my fashion consultants."

"Are you...here with someone?"

"Nah—I came stag. Wait a sec. Can girls come 'stag'? Shouldn't it be called 'doe'? Yeah, I like that better—I came doe."

He laughed and smiled at me again.

"You know what?" he asked, "Would you like to dance?"

"But...aren't you here with Ronnie?"

"Yes and...no. Listen, Ron...about Ronnie..." His face screwed up as he tried to collect his thoughts, but shook them off and eventually just shrugged. "Honestly, I don't care if I never see Ronnie again."

"That makes two of us."

He stared at the floor. He was obviously feeling ashamed of himself. When he looked back up at me, his eyes were pleading.

"Just...dance with me, Ron?"

I had to stifle a laugh at fate's comic timing, because the DJ had just dropped Roberta Flack's "The First Time Ever I saw Your Face."

"I'd love to."

He took my hand, and...

It was like something out of a dream, or something the fantasy me would have invented for herself, but this time it was as real as life gets. As we embraced and our eyes locked, I knew Bud *saw* me—he finally *really saw* **me**. And at that very moment it felt as if we were the only couple on the dance floor, sharing one singular id, with all our thoughts and dreams and feelings becoming a form of spooky matter, from here on out totally in sync and eternally connected. We were completely lost in each other as we spun together, with his big, warm hand gently holding me around my waist and mine resting lightly on his broad shoulder, swaying and turning, and nearly floating off of the floor to the music. This emotional rush should have scared me to death, because it felt even more powerful and stranger than my turning into Ronnie—but all every cell of my body felt this time was bliss.

The song ended. We let go and stood motionless for a second, still caught in each other's gaze, in some sort of wordless conversation of regrets and promises and "I'm sorries"—until the DJ dropped, of all things, "Stayin' Alive," by the Bee Gees, and we both burst out laughing.

So, I thought—*what the heck*—and launched into some Travolta-esque disco moves. If I was now going for total visibility, then why hold back?

Bud's eyes lit up in delighted surprise and he laughed anew, soon joining in with equal exaggerated gusto.

"Where'd you learn to dance like that?" he yelled over the music. "Did your weird brothers teach you this too?"

"Nah," I hollered back. "Didn't you know—even brainy girls watch American Bandstand."

As I twirled madly on one toe, I caught sight of Tanya Sweet waving, smiling, and shooting me a thumbs-up. No sooner did I catch that acknowledgement than I spotted the eerily-hooded Darleen Purdy weaving her way around the dance floor, slowly closing in on me again. From the other direction I saw Durk dancing with Lydia and very deliberately working his way toward Bud—that could only mean trouble. My eye then caught Mr. Randall, who was helping chaperone the dance, leering at *me* from the sidelines, then I spotted Eric Simon, who was with Josephine Kent, do a double-take when he saw me.

Well. My new visibility is certainly proving to be a mixed bag.

Right as the song ended, Durk deliberately bumped hard into Bud, setting him off balance and straight into me. We collided, but steadied each other.

We were fine but my orchid corsage was crushed. Durk laughed.

"Sorry, buddy, I thought you were a nerd," he mock-apologized, shooting me sneer, "which is... understandable, considering."

Lydia looked at me like she'd never seen me before—probably because she never honestly had—and blurted out, "Ooh...I *love* your dress!"

Durk shot her a "shut up" glare. He turned his glare at me next, and although I could tell I was still pretty much invisible to him, more of an obstacle or annoying impediment than an actual person, it dawned on me that there are some people in this world who will themselves into not seeing anything they don't want to see.

His glare was interrupted as a spotlight hit the platform up front and the room applauded Felicia Chao and Linda Burke, who walked to the microphone.

Well, it's the time you've all been waiting for, gang," Felicia announced. "The votes have been tallied and we have chosen our prom king and queen."

This was followed by more applause and a few whistles. Durk shot Bud an evil grin.

"Wait! **Hold on!** I want to make some late nominations for a **new** award!" Durk yelled out over the applause.

The room quieted. Linda Burke shaded her eyes from the spot to try to see who was yelling.

The spotlight panned the crowd and finally found Durk—and us.

Darleen was now only a few feet from me, but fortunately, the spotlight made her cower back.

"Now, I've known Bud Langston a long time," Durk boomed, "And when he told me he was bringing the prettiest girl in the school, I believed him! Well, I guess pretty is in the eye of the beholder, eh?!"

There were a few hesitant but snide snickers. Bud looked at me and I, at him.

"That's why I hereby nominate these two for The Dorkiest Couple At Talbot High!" he proclaimed, gesturing at us. "A question, Bud...is this the payoff for all those tutoring lessons she gave you? You must be in deeper debt than I thought!"

There was a burst of laughter and a few groans. Bud looked like he was going to slug Durk, so I gripped his arm to hold him back.

"Bud, don't. He's not worth it," I whispered.

"The least you could do is tell your date here it isn't a costume party! Or, maybe you thought this was a dog show?! Alls I knows is...!"

At this point things entered one of those surreal moments in life when everything seems to spin at both a hundred miles an hour and in slow motion. I tried to hold Bud back, but he broke loose and launched himself at Durk, throwing me back and out of the spotlight, where Darleen closed in, grabbing me, screaming, "Bite me!" The crowd laughed and started chanting, "Bite me! Bite me!" Bud and Durk knocked each other down, tussled and swore, everyone was either gasping or cheering or laughing or chanting, which made for a cacophony of generalized noise, and then...

I felt the twinge of Ronnie about to emerge again!

Utilizing my panicked adrenalin-rush, I shook loose of Darleen, leapt over Bud and Durk, nearly knocked down Lydia, and made a mad dash for the exit door, worming and elbowing my way through the crowd—somewhere in there I lost a shoe; with my body starting to morph and Darleen still hot on my tail, I didn't dare stop to retrieve it. When I glanced back, I saw Bud actually lift Durk over his head and throw him to the floor.

I hobbled down the exterior corridor and ducked into the main building.

It was dark and deserted.

My bust line started to swell and Ronnie giggled.

Shut up!

I heard footfalls outside. I quickly ducked into the first unlocked door I could find and quietly closed and latched it just as I heard someone else enter the building.

"Wheeeeeere aaaaaare yooooou?" Darleen sang out. Her footfalls continued down the main hallway and past my door.

I breathed a sigh of relief mixed with another one of Ronnie's inane giggles. I slapped a hand over my mouth.

Ronnie, don't even start! I'm still in control

here!

I turned around to discover that this doorway accessed a narrow stairwell and that's when I realized this must be the way up to the bell tower. I took off my other shoe to tip-toe up higher and higher, struggling at each step as I continued to lose control of my body. It continued its crunching and morphing as I continued climbing.

Ronnie was fully back and in charge again when we reached the top of the tower and saw the full moon low on the horizon, looking larger and brighter than it had all night.

She leaned on the ledge and stretched her arms out as if she'd wanted to reach out and grab it.

"So pretty!"

Then she noticed my crushed orchid corsage.

"Oh, darn."

She unpinned it, mourned its loss for a few seconds, and leaned over the tower rail to toss it away. She watched its flattened remains slowly spin and float down to land on the walkway below—right at Bud's feet.

Bud reached down to retrieve it. He glanced up.

I used every ounce of my will to successfully force Ronnie back from the rail so Bud couldn't see it was her.

Chapter Twenty-three

IF THE SHOE DOESN'T FIT...

Just when I thought I must have the worst luck on the planet, the last small cloud in the visible sky obscured the moon. Within a few minutes Ronnie had retreated back into whatever cellular off-switch DNA strand held her periodically captive.

I was myself again.

As I sat on a bench that must have been placed up there by some faculty smoker, with my hands on my knees, taking deliberate breaths, in and out, in and out, I tried not to panic. Tried to get a grip on things. Tried to think. I eventually sat up and toed at a couple of old cigarette butts while I wondered what to do next.

But I felt lost in a kind of fourth-dimensional limbo, floating all alone and completely untethered.

"The best laid schemes of mice and men..." I mumbled to myself, recalling Burns from Lit class, and to continue in my head with, "...leave us nought but grief and pain...."

That's when my tears began. I started shivering, partly because it was cold, but mostly from the intense feeling of utter hopelessness washing over me. I had no hanky or tissue, so, in desperation, I extracted the cotton balls from my remaining shoe and inspected them to confirm they were still clean enough to use to daub my eyes and cheeks dry.

I sat there, in the dark, all alone for—I have no idea how long. I had nothing left to think, feel, or give. No idea what to do next, or where to turn, no solutions, *nothing*. Just a hopeless, gaping pit in my stomach, and one ill-fitting shoe.

I heard the door downstairs creak open. That was followed by ascending footfalls on the stairs.

I hopped up and readied myself, holding my shoe aloft, heel out, as a weapon against Darleen.

Bud's head popped up in the stairwell instead.

I lowered my shoe and let out a shaky sigh of relief.

"We could have a duel," he offered, holding up my other shoe.

I sat again to weep anew.

Bud picked up both shoes and sat down next to me.

"Are you gonna be okay?"

"I'm so...*stupid*," I sobbed.

"What do you mean?"

I gestured to my dress and hair.

"This isn't me. I only did this...so you'd *see* me. So you'd *like* me."

"I already liked you."

"I was talking about..."

"I *know* what you're talking about. I'm not *completely* clueless—but I'm not as smart as you are. Okay? I admit it. It takes me longer to...process things. But, look Ron, I've known that you liked me for a long time. I just didn't fully admit to myself until tonight when we danced together and all...that I like you the same way. And have for a long time."

"I'm still not pretty enough to deserve you," I wept.

Bud laughed and shook his head.

"This is like a bad joke on both of us. Wanna know the truth, Ron? What kept me from admitting I had feelings for you is that *I* didn't feel good enough, or smart enough, to deserve *you*. That you were destined to marry some genius doctor like your dad and have a couple Mensa kids. And that my role was to be with one of the Ronnies of the world...kind of like that's the predetermined destiny of football players. You know? But I'm realizing it's a role I don't want—and that I have a choice."

I sobbed out a hopeful smile. He took off his coat and wrapped it around my shivering shoulders, then offered me a tissue. He put an arm gently around my waist and pulled me close to him for warmth.

"You're right you know—the make-up and all, yeah...okay, maybe that *isn't* really you? But none of that was what made me want to dance with you tonight. **None** of that is what made me...fall in love with you."

Bud got off the bench and dropped down on one knee to gently put my shoes back on for me. He rested back on his heel, looked up at me, and smiled, thinking.

"Oh, wait. I can fix this this whole evening. Hang on," he said, and reached in the pocket of his jacket to extract my flat corsage.

He clasped his hands together and held it out to me in a classic "proposal" pose.

"I should have done this in the first place—Rhonda Glock...will you go to the prom with me?"

I mocked a pouty smile as I took my sorry, decimated flower from him, and replied, "Um—sure. But I see two big problems with this proposal. One: we're already at the prom, and two..."

I paused to note the silence of the now deserted school.

"...sounds like the prom's all over?"

Our eyes met and we laughed together, both glad to finally release some of our tension with a joke.

"Look—I had it all so wrong," Bud continued, this time tears welling in his eyes. "Sure, Ronnie's cute...no, beautiful. And the power of her beauty fooled me into thinking there must be more to her than *just* that. With you, you're beautiful all the way down to your core. There's a depth and breadth and reality to it. With you, I don't feel manipulated..."

I laughed out a teary snort, interrupting him.

"Manipulated? You want to know the sad truth, Bud? I came to this dance dressed like this in a pathetic attempt to manipulate you into...kissing me," I confessed.

He looked confused.

I glanced up to see that last, lone cloud was about to move past the moon and expose it again.

"You'll understand soon enough."

Bud stood, pulled me up off the bench and into his arms.

"It's impossible to manipulate a willing participant."

Our lips meshed and we kissed, and nuzzled each other's necks, then kissed more, while the full light of the moon bathed the two of us in its cool blue glow.

When we got to the door at the bottom of the stairs, it hit me.

"Hey, how did you get in here? I locked this door!"

"That weird old janitor lady was waiting right outside it," he replied. "She said you were up here and had a key."

As we rounded the main stairwell, I heard a door creak open. Thinking it might be Darleen, I ducked behind Bud.

It was Lainey's door, but a tall, smartly dressed, attractive older woman I'd not seen before emerged.

A little Chihuahua puppy followed her. It dashed over to strop my leg and purr. I reached down to pick it up.

"Dinah? What a little cutie you are! But how..."

"Cats have nine lives," Lainey laughed. "Dinah is a lesson to us all. How we see ourselves is what really defines us and gives us our power. That, and maybe...a bit of magic."

"You look lovely," I complimented.

"As you see, I had my own reason for wanting to break the spell and set things right. I'm off to visit a widower who used to play football for Talbot High. One's never too old to hope for happy endings."

I crossed to her and gave her a warm hug. She hugged me back as Dinah licked my cheek. I handed Dinah to her.

"Well, wish me luck," Lainey sighed, "This time I'll try to do it without the magic."

"Good luck."

As Lainey walked away, Bud turned to me.

"I'm, like, *totally* confused here...who *was* that?"

"It's a long story—and you're not going to believe me, but it's all true, I swear..."

"Hold on—I'm starving. Do you wanna go somewhere for a **bite**?

I burst out laughing.

"What? What did I say?"

"If you only knew."

Gena stopped suckling and made a face, punctuating it with a burp. I laughed, which then made her smile back at me.

I did try to clearly and honestly explain everything to Bud over burgers that night after the prom, all those years ago, and, even though he swore he did, I was never convinced he really believed me. Things did change after that though—we were a "steady" couple, then fiancés, married, and were now parents.

Talbot High got used to seeing me, and seeing me with Bud. I actually became very good friends with Tanya Sweet and Felicia Chao after that.

And Darleen came back to school—when the spell was undone, she looked her old normal semi-cute self again, but never really got over the whole cheerleader thing. She got teased about it a lot. People would run up to her and yell, "Bite me!" Funny thing: I credit her with starting the expression, "Bite me!" that night at our prom, even though I can't really prove it categorically.

I retook my SATs and aced them with a perfect 1600—no further lives were ruined in the making of that score.

Bud walked in yawning and scratching at his bare chest. He leaned in and kissed my neck, but seeing the full moon in the window, he tilted my head to deliberately plant an emphatic one on my lips too.

Maybe he really *did* believe me.

Other Books By
AURELIO O'BRIEN
EVE

"EVE," transports us to a future both silly and stunning, as well as beautiful and brutal; one where all technology has been replaced by biology, by genetically designed Creature Comforts™.

The last functioning robot, Pentser, offended by this turn of events, induces its lonely human owner, Govil, a genetic designer for this world's sole facilitator, GenieCorp™, to violate every law of this new age and secretly create a companion: a normal, deliberately average woman, Eve.

Will Eve learn of her strange origins? Will GenieCorp™ track down the illicit pair, will Pentser's own mysterious plans come true, or will love indeed conquer all?

GENeration eXtraTERrestrial

Dr. Grace Brown, a government research scientist at ELF (The Extraterrestrial Life Forms Lab), must investigate a number of alleged abductees who believe they have been impregnated by aliens. To punish her boss for this unwanted assignment, Grace brings all these "nut-cookies" back to the lab for "further study." But the joke is on her when each gives birth to different and undeniably non-human offspring. This new generation extraterrestrial is as eccentric as their diverse Earth parents. The alien children cause pandemonium in the government, the courts, and the churches, as the world tries to cope with this unexpected new reality. Grace bonds with and adopts a tiny and brilliant alien boy, Charlie, whose mother died in childbirth. The others move in with their Earth parents and try to grow up as normally as an alien can.

Nature and nurture collide as these children and their families face issues of gender, race, religion, vegetarianism, politics, equality, adoption, alcoholism, love, divorce, sexuality, drug addiction, and fame. These ultimate outsiders must cope with parental love, sibling rivalries, peer pressure, and try to fit in, stand out, and make their way in the world, a world that is not really theirs. All the while one question is never far from their thoughts: will their absent and negligent space-parents return for them someday? Charlie makes it his personal mission to find out.

ABOUT THE AUTHOR

Aurelio O'Brien grew up in a piece of suburbia similar to his fictional Autumndale: Sunnyvale, California, before it became "Silicon Valley." He could have been described as a high school chameleon, floating from group to group and blending in unnoticed: choir, drama, brainy kids, student government, speech & debate, and the art geeks.

Aurelio's odd mix of talents led him to a successful career as an illustrator, animator, and graphic designer. After retiring from the world of visual storytelling, Aurelio expanded his skills to include the literary.

Now with **I Was A Teenage Cheerleader**, Aurelio explores discovering the self and our struggles coming of age in niches that work hard to define us for us before we have the full capacity to decide for ourselves who we really are and build niches all our own.

Printed in the USA
CPSIA information can be obtained
at www.ICGtesting.com
LVHW022255191124
797115LV00038B/984